FAMILY GHOULS

A Greek Ghouls Mystery

ALEX A. KING

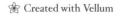

To the person who invented coffee

CHAPTER ONE

Old Vasili Moustakas was dead. I knew this because he was walking up the main beachfront street with his frank 'n' beans dangling out through the slit in his pajamas and no one else seemed to notice. They were the same blue-and-white checked bottoms he was wearing last month when he was hit by a car.

That had ended badly for everyone involved. Maria Stamatou ended up with a broken nose and a busted bumper, and Vasili Moustakas was nearly chopped in two. His walker had done zip to protect him.

Yeah, the oldest man on the island had definitely gotten the worst deal. And Maria? Well, she got a new nose which made her pretty happy, from what I hear. Her sister used to tell people that Maria could crack open a bottle of Heineken with her old nose. They say she probably ran old Kyrios Vasili down on purpose just so her father would buy her a new nose.

My name is Allie Callas (born Aliki—Alice—Callas) and I see dead people. In my experience, the dead aren't spooky. Most of the time they're weird and annoying. I live on Merope, a small island tethered to the ocean floor in the

Aegean Sea, wedged between Greece and Turkey. I'm thirty-one. Single (ask my mother and sister. They'll tell you; then they'll ask if you have a single brother, son, nephew, second cousin twice-removed, or a garbage man with a pulse and no wife). My parents are Greek, but we spent most of my childhood in the United States, besieged by phone calls and letters from both families, desperate to know why my parents cut out their hearts, pooped inside them, then set them on fire and put the fire out with skewers. When I was thirteen they succumbed to the pressure and moved back.

As a result, Merope isn't quite home. Don't get me wrong, it's a beautiful island. We have blazing summers and mild winters, with the occasional freak sprinkling of snow. It's also the biggest hotbed of sin outside of Mykonos and Athens; although you wouldn't know it if you were a regular tourist. You'd smile, take photographs of the quaint and charming scenery, including the pretty blue-and-white sign that reads Merope: population 21,271. You'd "oh" and "ah" over the ruins and the remnants of the olden days. You'd Facebook and Instagram our churches. Then you'd go home and tell people how lovely it was and how nice the people here are. It's all a carefully crafted and maintained image. The reality is much more gruesome ... once you rub through the first few layers.

As for me, I'm the woman people on Merope call when they want something done.

Need a impossible-to-find whatzit for your loved one's name day? I'm your woman. Have you been left out of the town gossip and alienated by your former friends? Call me and I'll find out why. Is your boyfriend cheating with his sleazy ex? I'll bring pictures. People are always willing to pay good money for help and information.

You'd think I'd be really unpopular at parties with a job like that, but on the contrary, people eat it up. They pull me aside on the street and tell me the kinds of things that would no one would believe if they were printed in a glossy gossip magazine. My business card reads Finders Keepers in a plain font, black on cream. Below that is my cell number, and right next to that is my email address.

(Contrary to the opinions of the local clergy, Merope has entered the computer age.)

Vasili Moustakas stood poised on the edge of the street, tethered fishing boats bobbing along the concrete dock not far behind him. He grinned his gummy grin and flipped his middle finger up at me. It's funny how cocky people get when they die. Death is the great anonymizer. It's easy to be a rebel when hardly anyone can see you.

From my bicycle seat I watched Vasili step out into the traffic. This time there was no screeching of brakes and crunching of metal as Maria's BMW had done when she collided with the old man's walker. Cars—three of them—zoomed right through him as he crossed the road. He shuffled over to my bicycle.

"Little Allie Callas," he said. "Have you got a smoke for an old man?"

"Smoking will kill you. And you just gave me the finger!"

His cackle burst into a phlegmy cough. I winced as he brought up an invisible lump of muck and spat it onto the pitted blacktop. "I wanted to see if you were watching me. Hey, take a look at this."

I made the mistake of looking down. He waved his *loukaniko*—his sausage—at me.

Ugh. Dirty old men are the worst, especially when they're dead.

Across the street my mark moved. It was Friday evening, and instead watching TV at home or cruising the promenade with friends I didn't have, I was minding someone else's business for a very reasonable fee. The blood had ceased its circulation in my thighs hours ago. My digital camera was at the ready, waiting for the moped rental guy to put so much as a pinky out of line. His wife, my client, was positive he was treating female customers to more than just a test ride.

She was probably right. They usually are.

Now it was up to me to snag the proof. Only Vasili Moustakas and his dead penis stood between me and the money shots.

I cleared my throat.

"I supposed you want me to move," he said, clearly miffed.

"I could take the picture right through you if you like."

"I slept with your *yiayia*."

"So did half of Merope," I said, unimpressed. My grandmother hadn't been exactly difficult in her youth. Word was that they used to call her *Frappe* because she went down easy on a hot summer day.

"She was terrible."

"You know what else is terrible? Dead people. You're annoying."

He mumbled something unintelligible and probably obscene, and shuffled aside. The camera clicked and I got my first shot of Dimitri Vlahos, who owned the most popular moped rental business on the island, getting into a new BMW with Maria Stamatou and her new nose. It might have been innocent except he had his hand fastened around one of her breasts—a recent purchase.

I got rid of the elderly sausage swisher and followed Dimitri and Maria to the Hotel Hooray (yes, that's its real name), a kilometer past the village limits. I was on my bicycle but following them wasn't a chore; there was only one hotel this far out of the village, at least on the western edge.

They rented a room by the hour and made my job easier by leaving the curtains of the first floor room open a fraction; just enough space for my camera to snap thirty perfect pictures of Dimitri playing hide-the-souvlaki with Merope High School's most popular student.

They weren't alone in the squalid room. In Ancient Greece, long before Merope became Merope, a brothel stood in this exact spot. Two of its workers still lived here. They'd burned to death in a fire and therefore had issues with walking toward the light. Right now they were whooping and hollering, egging the oblivious couple onwards.

"Can we really call that a *poutsa*?"

"I believe that is illegal, unless you do it with a donkey."

Dimitri and Maria kept on going. If they only knew.

Medium, channel, psychic, witch, necromancer; those are all fancy names for something I'm not. I'm just a normal woman. Fifty-something kilos (hundred-and-twenty pounds, if we're talking American measurements) of brunette mediocrity, who happens to see ghosts walking around like regular people. Only they're not really regular anymore. It's like something weird happens after they die and they go wherever the dead go for those forty days they allegedly spend wandering the earth. The Greek Orthodox Church believes that during those forty days immediately after death, the deceased roam around their homes, checking in one loved ones, scoping out their graves. But as far as I know the Church is wrong and the dead don't show up until the forty-day memorial has been and gone. And when they do, their inhibitions have often vanished, and more often than not their annoying personality traits are magnified times a hundred. If you watched me on a day-to-day basis there's a good chance you'd see me muttering out the side of my mouth like a lunatic.

I'm really not. That's just me trying to be discrete when the ghosts get chatty.

With my next paycheck trapped in a memory stick, I left Maria to her souvlaki.

There are two supermarkets in my part of the village, each owned by one of the Triantafillou brothers: the Super Super Market and the More Super Market. I frequent More Supermarket because it's the closest to my apartment, even though it's the less super of the two—or at least that's the story I tell myself. Sometimes rats scurry by. Sometimes it's spiders. Last October I caught one of the employees rubbing his wiener in a bag of chocolates. I no longer buy bagged sweets. The More Super Market is dimly lit, and more of its shelf space is devoted to dust than any actual product, but it's not haunted, so it's got that going for it.

Gripping a short list scribbled in my barely legible hand, I hurried around the store and stuffed groceries into a basket: feta, mortadella, shampoo, and a bottle of milk for my neighbor and friend, Olga Marouli.

I emptied my basket onto the counter. Stephanie Dolas, checkout chick and a chatterbox, had something to say.

"Maria Stamatou has got a new boyfriend," she said, and waited expectantly, flicking a nail against her buck teeth.

Stephanie would crap her pants if she knew what was in my handbag. "Any idea who?"

She shrugged and dropped the groceries into a plastic sack. "I think it's an older man. Maybe a teacher."

"That's a bit dangerous, isn't it? She's what, seventeen?"

"Eighteen. Why does she get all the good guys?"

I shook my head and gave her a twenty euro note. "Believe me, you're better off with the guys your own age. They're much less complicated."

She gave me the what-do-you-know-you're-like-old look. Give me a break. At thirty-one my toes weren't even creeping toward the grave yet.

I took the change, thanked her, and picked up the bag with two fingers while I juggled coins, notes, and the receipt.

My home is two blocks away from the More Super

Market. The apartment building is well cared for. White, like most buildings here. Three floors. A pretty garden in the small courtyard, and a burbling fountain that always reminds me that my bladder is shrinking with each passing year.

Mine is one of the six apartments in the building. I'd been living in number 202 for five years, and I didn't feel like moving any time soon.

Olga Marouli (Kyria Olga, I called her. Mrs Olga. Forget the appropriate honorific at your own peril. You'll be a pariah for the rest of your life. Nobody forgets anything here, except their own personal scandals; and when they do there is always someone helpful around to remind them) shares the second floor with me. Her apartment is a mirror image of my own, with better furnishings and the homey smell of gardenias and vanilla. She's one of the few people I call friend. I don't have too many of those. The nature of my work contributes significantly to my suspicious and untrusting nature. Trust no one; isn't that what Fox Mulder said?

On the way back to my bicycle, I pulled my light coat closed. The nights were shorter now, and winter was preparing to show up for its annual vacation in the northern hemisphere. Still, it was only October; winter wouldn't be arriving for another few weeks. But this evening I could definitely feel that subtle shift that tells you that summer is done kissing you goodbye.

———

It took all of ten seconds to shove the groceries in my fridge and crumple the plastic bag into a wad. I shoved it up inside a bag holder shaped like a grandmother. As always, I apologized for sticking the bags up her butt, although she hadn't complained yet.

The ceiling creaked. I raised a glass of water in a toast; my neighbor was getting laid. Again. I'd never met him but I'd seen him from a distance. He was the one of a handful of people in town I knew very little about, but then he'd only been living above me for a month or two. So far I knew that he had a spectacular body and he got laid a lot.

After wiping the glass I shoved it back in the cupboard and scooped up the bottle of milk Kyria Olga asked me to bring.

I stepped out of my door and paused.

Her door was ajar.

Was it that way when I came home? My head had been so far up my rear end, thinking about Dimitri and Maria, that I couldn't be certain.

In the minuscule gap between heartbeats, the tiny hairs on back of my neck tingled. Blood swooshed through my ears, turning me temporarily deaf.

My gut hoisted a Jolly Roger.

I sat the milk down in the hallway. In slow motion my leg extended so that the tip of my shoe pressed against the door. A small push opened the door wide.

"Kyria Olga, are you decent?" I didn't want to scare her if she was sitting on the toilet.

Hand on the pepper spray I'd acquired from a tourist of dubious reputation, I went in.

Time slowed to a drunken crawl.

My lungs sucked in deep swallows of air. It should have kept me calm. It didn't. I wanted to run and pee at the same time. My mind shoved back at the adrenalin coursing through my blood. Back flat against the walls, I crept through the apartment. My eyes darted from side to side, looking for signs of trouble.

Something resembling a mass of lilac cotton-candy spilled out at floor level from behind the L shaped kitchen cabinets.

My heart fell down through my shoes, landing on the floor with a *thud!*

Not cotton candy.

Time recovered, picking up its pace. I raced over to the form of Olga Marouli lying spread-eagle on her gray and white marble floor. I didn't need to touch her to know she was gone. Waxen skin. Blue lips. In death, the wrinkles had dropped from her face, leaving her skin as smooth as a kewpie doll. Her legs were akimbo, as though she had buckled at the knees. A necklace of bruises marred her neck, a color that complimented the lilac rinse in her hair, I thought, half hysterical. Another bruise, barely a smudge, left a brush of color on her weatherbeaten cheek.

Olga Marouli wasn't just dead; she'd been murdered.

CHAPTER TWO

An eternity passed while I waited for the boys in black to arrive. I used my time wisely, wearing a groove into the marble in the hallway between the two apartments.

"Allie?" A voice interrupted my reverie. The young cop with the buzzcut and angular frame was Gus Pappas. I didn't know him well but I could smell the fear-tinged excitement on him; this was his first murder.

"Hey, Pappas." My voice sounded foreign. Something dark inside me had taken over, forcing me to cope. "Kyria Olga is in her kitchen, over there."

The cop and his team disappeared into the apartment followed by the island's coroner, Panos Grekos, a brusque man whom I was vaguely acquainted with. His dead mother hung around the *periptero*—newsstand—screaming like a banshee whenever her son stopped to purchase Playboy magazine. Grekos isn't smart enough to score his porn for free on the internet like the rest of civilization, or maybe he just enjoys sticking it to his dead mama. He has the body of a bear and the head of a fox—at least that's what rumors say. I've never seen his place.

Thirty seconds later, Pappas ran back out. "It's my first dead body," he said, and sprayed puke on the marble.

"Mine too," I said and threw up in solidarity. I see the dead on a regular basis, but not until a good forty days after they've vacated their bodies, and never when they're my friends.

"Allie," Pappas said, inspecting the mess. "Did you have corn?"

I didn't stick around.

Nothing had changed in my apartment. It was exactly as I had left it. Simple, spartan with the bulk of my earnings put into the electronics that made my job easier. There was no physical evidence that a murder had occurred just meters away. Yet it all seemed different. Nothing looked like it belonged. Oooh, maybe this was one of those parallel universes.

No?

I made it as far as the kitchen before sliding to the floor. I drew my knees tightly against my chin and hugged them hard. Each time the image of my friend and neighbor's dead body floated into focus, I shoved it away and tried to concentrate on who might have done this to her, and why.

Olga Marouli. Seventy something. Kind, with a wicked sense of humor. She did sarcasm like other people do breathing. She was widowed some years earlier, before I'd moved into the building, and saw pretty much nothing of her three children and grandchildren. She never complained about money, but if she had cash to spare it wasn't reflected in her possessions. As far as I knew, her social life was marginally better than my own farcical attempts. She attended a knitting group on Saturdays, played Bingo down at the Merope Coffee House on Tuesday nights, and repented in church on Sundays, before rushing out to the church courtyard to swap gossip. She regularly knocked on my door, a basket of meat swinging on her arm, offering to share her Bingo winnings. I always refused. And she always barged in and stuck several packets of meat into my freezer. My retaliation was preparing dinner for two.

Oh God, I was going to miss her.

Pain gripped me and gave me a bone crushing squeeze.

"It is very nice that you are grieving, but really, you should quit moping around and find out who killed me."

My chin jerked up off my knees. My jaw dropped as I took in the voice's owner.

Olga Marouli stood in front of me, hands on hips, transparent, and—judging by her expression—extremely annoyed about the whole death situation.

My eyelashes fluttered as I scrambled to process what I was seeing. I see ghosts all the time, but this was different. This one was *personal*. Just minutes ago I'd discovered her body on the kitchen floor, and now she was back, way before her forty days was up.

Kyria Olga spoke again. "How am I supposed to watch my shows now?"

I blinked again and considered soiling my underwear. It sounded like a solid plan until I remembered that the person cleaning them would be ... well ... me. Smart people don't create messes for themselves, and I like to think my parents didn't raise an idiot.

So I went with choice number two and blurted out, "Are you sure you're really dead? Because I just saw you a moment ago lying on the kitchen floor. Isn't this kind of sudden? I didn't realize ghosts could happen so quickly."

Kyria Olga drew herself up to her full four-feet-eleven inches inside her black dress. As in life, her ghost was wearing black knee-high stockings, black slippers, and a black apron. For Greek widows, black is a lifetime commitment. The lilac-tinted beehive added another three inches.

"*Po-po*, what kind of question is that? I always thought you were a good girl. Now are you going to find my murderer or not?"

I gulped as she levitated above the marble tile. "You weren't this bossy when you were alive," I said. It was hard to make small talk with a friend while their body was being hauled away in a body-bag not twenty meters away.

"Yes, I was."

Maybe she was just a hallucination

Don't be stupid, Allie, I told myself, *you see this kind of thing all the time.*

"How did you come back so fast?"

"You're good at discovering things." She waved a hand in agitation. "Go and investigate!"

Then with a poof and a small pinging sound, she was gone.

It's a lie, my mind told me. *They never come back this fast.*

Don't be stupid, the other voice said. *If she's a figment of your imagination, then why is she so cranky?*

Wouldn't you be cranky if you woke up dead? a third voice asked.

Madness, that was it, I was going insane. Eventually my parents would have no choice but to lock me up in an institution with an IV of thorazine dripping into my veins. Although, come to think of it, besides the whole finding my friend dead thing, and seeing her ghost an unprecedented few moments later, I didn't feel too insane. No more than usual anyway.

Maybe that's one of the signs of being crazy: you don't actually realize you're completely nuts. Only the people around you notice. And they give you funny sideways looks, only you'll be oblivious on account of being crazy, and all the while you'll go on talking to invisible people and chewing on the shutters while people shake their heads and whisper things like, "Stay away from the crazy woman," and, "I hope she's sterile."

I picked up the phone and dialed the one person who was bitter and twisted enough to coddle me back into reality.

My sister Toula.

———

Toula showed up precisely fifteen minutes after my desperate call. She arrived in a whirlwind of domesticity, wiping, dusting, and general fussing.

My skin itched.

I wanted to fling dirt around the room.

It was our parents' joke on the world to raise two daughters so different that we almost required a translator to communicate. A few weeks earlier our parents announced that they were "abandoning" us to travel around the world on a fancy cruise ship. Toula and I were on our own for the next few months.

If we both survived.

Give us a personality test, we would answer every last question differently. But to look at us, there was no doubt we're sisters. Same dark brown hair, same dark eyes eyes, same slim build. We're even the exact same 1.70 meters (5'7") and size thirty-nine shoe. Toula has a bigger chest and she never lets me forget it. I always tell her gravity loves to take its pound of flesh and drag it to knee level.

"Want me to fix you some tea?" Toula called out from the kitchen.

She was getting a kick out of babying me. Upon arrival, she'd pushed me onto the sofa and wrapped a blanket around my shoulders. Now she was fussing around in the kitchen, doing who knows what. Probably scrubbing my cupboards.

"That would be fine," Even to my own ears my voice sounded distant and tinny.

Rattling ensued, then she returned with a glass in hand. "I don't know how you manage to survive. There is nothing in your kitchen. A person needs a balanced diet. Meat. *Horta*. Cheese."

"Nobody needs *horta*."

Horta are greens. Or at least that's what centuries of Greek women tell me. But you can't fool me; I know weeds when I see them.

She shoved the glass at me. "Drink this. It will help until the water boils. Do you have any milk?"

"In the hall," I said, and sipped the liquid. Ouzo, neat, and it tasted like decent stuff, not the cheap paint thinner I occasionally buy when I'm expecting company. My sister had brought the bottle with her. Nice.

Toula's question was etched on her face.

I drained the glass. "Never mind, I'll get it." Blanket wrapped around my shoulders, I shuffled out to the hall and found the milk right where I'd left it. Yellow tape formed a barrier across Kyria Olga's doorway. The door was open and the sounds of an evidence hunt filtered out into the hallway.

I didn't think Kyria Olga would mind me taking the milk, although I should have thought to ask her about it when she came to visit. Hopefully it didn't have dead people cooties. Not that I was really worried, the cooties would just add to the flavor.

"Cooties," I giggled, still in shock, and sat the container on the counter.

Toula looked horrified. "Did you just steal milk from a dead woman?"

"Steal? No. More like borrowing on permanent basis." I shuffled into the kitchen, blanket still clutched tightly around my shoulders, and snatched up the liquor bottle. Two fingers of ouzo sloshed into a glass. Perfect. For starters.

"Kyria Olga?" I called out. "Is it okay if I take your milk?"

She didn't magically appear. Just my imagination after all. Talking to her earlier must have been a sign of shock, and the ouzo was taking care of that.

I gulped some more medicine down, feeling the heat in my throat and belly. Maybe if I drank enough of this stuff I'd forget the sight of Olga Marouli's lifeless body.

"Allie ..."

Uh oh, my sister that that look on her face; The disapproving I-smell-poop one.

"Yeeess?"

"It's disrespectful to make jokes about the dead."

My eyes rolled upward. "Trust me, she doesn't care. She's dead. What's she going to do? Reanimate her corpse and eat my brains?"

Toula's nose wrinkled. She popped the foil lid off the milk and sniffed. If it had cooties, she'd know.

She poured the milk into one of the two mugs I own that don't have chipped rims. It passed her muster, or at least it was fit for me to drink, so I went back to the couch, tea in one hand, ouzo in the other. I was miffed that she hadn't brought me any of her *koulourakia,* those hard Greek cookies that smell like oranges and taste like a crumbly kind of heaven. The woman might be a pain, but she can really bake. I would have given my spleen for a few of her *koulourakia.* After all, I wasn't exactly using my spleen. And what was a spleen for, anyway?

Toula hovered by the sofa.

"Sit," I said. She was making me nervous.

"I can't stay," she said. "I have to clean my kitchen."

"God knows I wouldn't want to stand between you and your kitchen."

She hovered at the door like a bad smell. "I'm sorry about Kyria Olga."

"You're sorry. I'm sorry ..."

"You're taking this hard. It's not as though she was family."

"Family isn't always blood."

She took a deep breath, like she was psyching herself up for something big. "Is this about Andreas?"

Yeah, that was about as big as it got.

I couldn't stop the flinch or the dull ache that always followed when anyone mentioned his name. Andreas was my fiancé. He'd left me standing alone one night in the Super Super Market while I was ordering bacon at the deli counter. I hadn't seen him since.

"Kiss my butt, Toula."

"Allie ..."

"Just go. I'll be fine. I'm the self-sufficient one, remember?" My words were cruel, but true. And I regretted them as soon as I said them. It was always that way between us.

"Fine. Fine." Pain flickered in her eyes. "There's some soup in the fridge for you. Just put it in the microwave for three minutes on high." She shuffled from foot to foot as though trying to think of something else to say, then pecked me on the forehead. The door slammed moments later.

I squinted at the ancient soldier on the ouzo bottle. I opened and closed each eye one at a time and made him hop around on the bottle. Small things amuse small and desperate minds.

It's just me and you, you handsome old devil.

Opa!

In one smooth move, I drained the glass. Then I abandoned the glass and jumped straight into swilling the clear liquid straight out of the bottle. It burned all the way to my toes. I hobbled over to my phone dock and pushed play.

Led Zepplin. *Perfect.*

My brain clicked *off*. My mouth clicked *on*.

Two verses into an off-tune sing-a-long to *Stairway to Heaven*, I heard a voice.

"Keep drinking. That will really help me." Kyria Olga's voice was lemon-sour with a twist of acetone. So was her face. Both of them.

I opened and closed each eye, making Kyria Olga's faces dance.

"Don't have to ask me twice." With a small toast gesture, I tipped the bottle up and swallowed. The ouzo was perfectly smooth now. The skin inside my throat was numb. "My body, my apartment, my ouzo. And you," I said pointedly, "are a figment of my sober imagination. Which means you shouldn't even be here, since I'm no longer sober. In fact you shouldn't be here at all. Not for another forty days, anyway."

"Where else would I be? I live here."

"I don't think 'live' is the word you're looking for—not now. And as far as I know, the dead don't come back until after their forty days are up."

"Then how am I here, eh?" She floated off into the kitchen. "Is this my milk?"

Oh hell, I knew I should have asked. "It's mine now. You don't exactly need it."

"You don't know that," she said, sniffing.

"Course I do. You don't see dead people posing for those Got Milk? advertisements, and there's a good reason for that. Calcium is a moot point for you now. You don't have bones. Or teeth. I bet you've even given up eating."

"*Po-po*, shame on you making fun of my condition." Kyria Olga floated off again, this time right through the front door. A moment later she was back. "You have got a visitor," she said.

"Yes, and you keep coming back," I said dryly. "Don't they

have medication for this? Because I could really use some right now. Preferably in an I.V. drip."

"No. Another one." Her head popped back through the door. "Oh-la-la, he is a handsome one."

Before I could protest, the doorbell chimed. I grudgingly dragged myself to the door and peered through the peephole. Handsome? The Elephant Man reincarnate filled the lens, hands shoved deep into the pockets of his jeans.

He was probably from one of those church groups that believes accosting you in your home will make you susceptible to conversion. Anyone who tries to sell another religion to the Greek Orthodox Church's flock is fighting with both hands tied behind their backs.

"Are you selling something? Because if you are, I don't want any," I said, trying not to sound like a drunk.

"Aliki Callas? I'm Detective Samaras. I need to ask you a few questions."

I was impressed that the local police department was hiring the handicapped. Very progressive in a country that often likes to make believe it's still the 1960s. *Hic.* Poor man, with that face.

"O-o-h," I said enthusiastically. "Twenty questions, that's a fun game. Come in, you can go first." I unlocked the door, unhooked the chain and opened wide.

My gaze hit his chest and began to climb ... and climb. A hundred and ninety centimeters (six-two and change). An overabundance of shoulders and chest. Dark hair. Strong jaw. Full lips. Hmm, not so deformed after all—although he did have four hazel eyes ... or was it six?

For some inexplicable reason he looked puzzled.

I flipped him a little wave instead of holding out my hand. He didn't seem interested in shaking it anyway.

"Can I come in."

"Be my guest." I chased up my invitation with a verse of *Beauty and the Beast's Be Our Guest.*

He sat and pulled a notebook from his black leather jacket pocket.

"Am I supposed to clap?" he said.

"No. I know I'm amazing." I crossed my ankles and sat primly on the couch. It took all my muscle control to remain upright.

"You found Olga Marouli?"

"Um, animal, vegetable, or mineral?"

"Your full name please."

"You're being terribly unfun."

His expression was stone, and that wasn't the ouzo talking. "Your full name."

"Allie Callas. Wait—Aliki Callas. Everyone calls me Allie. People only call me Aliki when I'm in trouble."

"Really?"

"Would I lie about that?"

He scribbled something in his notebook.

Kyria Olga floated over and craned her neck over his shoulder, inspecting him. "He is very sexy. You could do worse —and have."

"Shh!"

The detective looked up. "Did you say something?"

"I was talking to my friend."

He turned around and looked into the kitchen. "I don't see anyone here but us."

"That's because she's dead," I whispered.

Kyria Olga rolled her eyes. "Really, Allie? Really?"

"That's why I'm here," he said. "You found her?"

"Yesh." Uh-oh, I was nearing the point of alcoholic-no return.

"Do you have a key or was the door open?"

I waved a hand vaguely in the direction of the hallway

where a series of hooks held my keys, my purse, and a sorry-looking umbrella. "My keys are over there."

"Olga Marouli's keys?"

"No, *vlakas* ... why would I have her keys?"

Fabulous. I was vaguely aware that I'd just called him stupid, but I couldn't stop myself.

"So you don't have her keys?"

"No."

"So the front door was open?"

"Yesh." My chin bobbed vigorously. Smashed or not, I was eager to cooperate with the six-eyed policeman.

Perched on the edge of the armchair now, Kyria Olga pointed at the cop's notepad. "He is writing something about your drinking problem."

Who me? "I am not a drunk! I'm just upset about finding a dead person!"

Kyria Olga rolled her eyes.

Detective Samaras was more forgiving. "Under the circumstances, I would be drinking too. In fact, when I get back upstairs, I'll be knocking back a beer."

"Upshtairs?

"We're neighbors." He indicated upwards.

"This is fun, yes?" Kyria Olga said, clapping her hands like a small, excitable child.

"You're the one with the revolving bedroom door?" I leaned forward. "How do you manage it? You can tell me. Is it energy drinks?"

His eyebrows shot skyward, so high they nearly disappeared into his hairline. He snapped the notebook shut, and stood. "I think it would be in both our interests if we continued this tomorrow." Three steps later, he was rattling around in my kitchen cupboards. He returned moments later with a glass and two aspirin. "Open your mouth."

"Is it a roofie? Because I don't take roofies from strangers."

He snorted. "I'm not going to do the airplane, so open up now."

My mouth fell open, out of surprise mostly. He popped the two aspirin on my tongue and shoved the glass into my hand.

"You're going to feel like dog *skata* tomorrow." His lips curved into a tiny smug smile. If I was sober I'd have kicked his butt. If I was more intoxicated, I might have kissed it.

He returned the glass to the kitchen. "I know Merope isn't a place where people don't always lock their doors, but lock your door tonight," he said, and went out the same way he'd come in.

In slow, viscous, liquid motion my body flopped horizontally on the couch. My vision doubled as my eyelids fluttered.

Then I blinked.

A ginger cat was scratching behind an ear with one foot, right there on my coffee table. I stared at him until he looked up at me, then I wished I hadn't. Poor thing had an overbite that would make my dentist run out to buy another yacht.

His head dipped, and he got busy licking his balls.

Lucky devil.

CHAPTER THREE

Death had taken a vacation in my mouth. He'd set up camp on my tongue, and left behind a coat of fur and sour ouzo stench as a reminder of my solo drinking binge the night before. If that wasn't enough, a killer headache cleaved my skull in two, and my eyeballs were the victims of a sharp stick poking, followed by hot pepper sauce eye drops. All this before I tried to move a muscle.

Really, some days I just had all the luck.

I heaved my body sideways and with a plop and an ominous crunch, landed on the floor. The painstaking task of getting to the kitchen began.

Like a caterpillar, I dragged myself on my elbows, butt rising in the air then falling as my knees tried to gain traction on the marble tile ... and failed.

For a normally sensible woman, I was a pathetic mess.

My own stupid fault.

Suddenly yesterday came pouring back into my head, filling it to the brim with grief. My friend was gone—murdered—and I was on the fast track to the psych ward.

I wiped a hand across my mouth. At least I think it was *my* hand.

In one move, devoid of all grace, I rolled over and flopped on my back. A yelp popped out of my mouth.

Kyria Olga was back and inspecting my face.

"My Virgin Mary, you look like the wrong end of a donkey. No wonder you're not married," she said.

"You're still dead?" I shuffled a little further toward the kitchen.

Her misty shoulders heaved. "Yes, and it is a rather strange sensation. Turn on the TV, eh? I am missing my shows." Her body might be deceased, but her penchant for trash television was eternal.

"What did your last servant die of? I'm not exactly mobile yet."

"Disobedience."

What the hell, I'd ride this out and see where my delusion took me. I was too hung over to fight it, anyway.

"Fine, I'll do it, just this once. But I have to warn you, research shows that stuff rots your brain."

"What brain? I am dead. I do not need my brain."

Right. Made sense. "If you're really a ghost, why are you here?"

"I told you, I want you to find out who killed me."

"I don't mean that. I mean why are you here so soon."

"I came as soon as I could. Why?"

My knees drew up again, and I tried to sit. This time it worked, although the world shook and spun. "It usually takes longer for the dead to come back. I'm not sure why, but I figure it's some kind of adjustment period."

"Oh, that," she said, waving her hands through the remote. "We can come back immediately if we have unfinished business."

"Which you do?"

"Murder most heinous. I wish you had told me sooner about your unusual gift. We could have had fun."

I ignored her. It was time to try that standing thing.

Like a wobbly toddler, I grabbed the counter lip and heaved. Finally, I was on two feet. For now.

Using hidden energy reserves, I poured some water. I guzzled two glasses before carrying a third back to my makeshift bed on the sofa. Kyria Olga waited, tapping a crepe-soled ghost-slipper on the floor. I clicked the remote and fell back into the soft cushions of the sofa. I prayed for my own death.

No more ouzo.

Ever.

Until the next time.

We sat in silence for a time, until I began to perk up slightly and finally asked, "Any chance you saw who killed you?"

"No."

"You were there and you didn't see them?"

"Everything is hazy, which is completely normal, or so they tell me."

"They?"

"The Council of the Formerly Living."

"There's a council?"

"A council with rules and regulations. They say they do not like us mixing with the living too much. Our involvement has to be peripheral. That is what they said in orientation."

I'd been conversing with the dead since I was a kid, and this was the first I'd heard about rules and a council.

"So why are you sitting here watching soap operas? Doesn't the council of dead people frown on that too?"

"Council of the Formerly Living."

"Council of the Formerly Living." I shut my eyes tight. Perhaps when I opened them again she'd be gone.

"I am here," she said, "so you can investigate my murder. But since I am here anyway, I do not see any harm in watching a little television."

I sighed deeply. Even that made me feel tired. "It would help if you at least gave me a list of people who might want to kill you. Assuming of course that it wasn't a random serial killer."

"So you can pass it on to the police? *Pshaw*."

"Olga Marouli, I find things. I'm not a policewoman. I deal in infidelity, china plates, and lost puppies. Murder is way out of my league."

"If it is a question of money ..."

"It's not. The police are liable to frown on it if I snoop while they're trying to conduct their investigation. I may even be a person of interest at this stage just because I found your ... uh ... found you."

The stars of daytime television were forgotten. My friend twiddled her fingers. Her lower lip quivered. "Then I will haunt you until you find my killer."

"I'll contact the Greek Orthodox Church and get an exorcist."

Her eyes narrowed. Game on. "Then I will tell the entire Formerly Living community that you are the person to come to when they need help."

"You wouldn't dare!" I yelped.

"Maybe I would. Maybe I would not." Her eyes narrowed more, until they became almond slivers. She meant business.

It was official. My butt had been handed to me on a platter, a bright red delicious apple wedged between my cheeks.

Virgin Mary, I hoped there wouldn't be stuffing.

Frankly, I didn't need this. I wanted to grieve for Olga Marouli, not argue the minutiae of police jurisdiction with her ghost. The police could do their job, catch her killer, and put him behind bars where he could catch rats for dinner and beg for toilet paper. Greece's prisons, like the rest of Greece, are hurting for funds. So corners get cut. Corners. Food. Toilet paper.

The police.

An uncomfortable feeling began to metastasize inside me. A vague memory hammered at the haze in my head.

"Did anyone come here last night?"

Her lavender head swiveled back to the flickering screen. "Your sister. She made you some tea. She used my milk too …"

I exhaled. Sweet relief. I'd do something nice for my sister later, like buy her a real personality.

"… and that policeman who lives above you, of course. He gave you some pills and tucked you in. You should marry him. You could use a man."

"So he really was here?"

"Of course."

"Did I make a complete fool of myself?"

Of course I did, which is why I had a sinking feeling in my stomach.

Kyria Olga glanced at her bare wrist. "Is that the time? I have to go. I have a thing to do with some other formerly living people." She *poofed* away, leaving me alone with the hangover from hell and a burning sensation in my cheeks.

———

By noon I felt halfway human. I'd done a repair job in the shower, washing life back into my weak body. With fresh jeans, a clean sweater (black, because I was in mourning for Kyria Olga) and a touch of lip-gloss and mascara, I felt like I could be accepted in public without being bounced off the island.

Before running out the door to my meet with my desperate client, I hooked the camera up to my computer and uploaded the photographs I'd snapped yesterday. One by one proof of the moped peddler's duplicity slid out of the printer in full-blown glossy color.

I selected ten of the best and slid thcm into a manila envelope, along with my invoice and a detailed report of how I'd spent my time and my client's money. Kyria Vlaho had paid a generous retainer, eager to catch her philandering husband mid-nookie. Now that my work was completed, she only owed forty-three euros. At times, obtaining those last few dollars out of clients could be like trying to squeeze mois- ture out of a handful of Lemnos's sand; I didn't think this would be one of those times. Kyria Vlaho would just add the forty-three euros to her generous divorce settlement. I just hoped the wrong wife didn't take too much of her wrath out on Maria Stamatou. The poor girl had already bought one new nose this year.

Fifteen minutes remained until my appointment. I could make it in five, with enough time left over to order a latte before she showed.

A scratching at the front door made me jump. The marmalade cat was back and digging at the tile. Now that I was sober I remembered him from last night. Huh. I guess he hadn't come out of the ouzo bottle after all.

"Hey, little kitty." I crouched and waggled my fingers. He remained unimpressed for a whole second before trotting over to see what I was offering. I reached out to touch him ... and missed.

Huh. Ghost cat.

Some ghosts are more solid than others. Usually the longer they've been dead the more solid they become. This has no effect on their convenient ability to walk through walls. This cat was the most opaque spirit I'd ever seen. I could almost count his ratty little tufts of fur. He was a cute kitty ...for the ugliest cat I'd ever seen in my life.

A sharp knock made me jump. Not my apartment. I played it cool in case Olga's killer had come back for seconds, and looked to my apartment to get his kicks.

The knocking stopped, replaced by a scuffling sound, like a rat trying to scratch through wood.

Barely breathing, I raised my eye to the peephole.

CHAPTER FOUR

"Olga? Are you home?" A deep smooth voice penetrated the door. My shoulders relaxed. Although I'd never been introduced to the white-haired man, I recognized him as a regular visitor to Olga Marouli's apartment. Tall. Thin. Confident. In his youth he would have been a handsome man, and the remnants of those good looks held on tight even now as old age was fighting hard to rip them away. His jaw was defined and strong underneath the slight softening of the skin and the folds below his chin. Eyes of clear brown looked out through wrinkled lids and his hair was still firmly attached to his head. Probably that made him a catch among the retired set.

Evidently he hadn't heard about Kyria Olga's demise. I hated to be the bearer of tragic news. I took a deep breath and opened the door.

"Where is Olga? I saw the tape..." he trailed off.

I looked the door to 201. The police were long gone, and the door shut tight, but the yellow taped remained. The vomit, I noticed, was gone.

"I'm so sorry, she's gone."

His face underwent a transformation, from solid to melting point in seconds. He was going to break down right there in front of me.

Help. I've never been good at providing comfort. I deal in facts, not emotions. Quietly and calmly I gave him the facts as I knew them and hoped it would suffice.

Slowly, his face stabilized, preserving his male pride. "So it is true. I read it in the paper and thought it had to be a mistake. They know who did it?"

"No, not yet."

He pulled a card from his shirt pocket. "Soon as you hear anything, pick up the phone, please?" I pocketed the card and watched as he shuffled down the hall, a broken man.

I knew a little about the man. Stavros Psaris--that was his name—and the late Kyrios Maroulis had been fast friends since the Regime of the Colonels. After his friend died, Stavros Psaris visited regularly to check in on his friend's widow. I don't pretend to be brilliant, but in my line of work, reading a person is important. Sometimes an expression can give you the clue you need to push forward and break the case. Right now, that little voice inside me was jumping up and down, and I'd wager it was right: Stavros Psaris had been unrequitedly in love with Olga Marouli.

———

"I am going to kill him!"

"No—no killing."

"Can I cut off his *poutsa?*"

"No cutting."

"What about making him sorry his jackal of a mother brought him into this world?"

"You can do that if you want. Just no killing or cutting."

Kyria Vlaho snatched the photos from my hands with the

gleeful giggle of a woman whose instincts had proved correct. She scribbled a check for forty-three dollars in her bold cursive hand and practically danced out of the coffee shop, incriminating evidence tucked in her purse, leaving me to flip through a newspaper and sip the remainder of my coffee.

Once upon a time, I harbored fantasies about running my business out of an office. Nothing fancy, just something cozy and sunlit, where clients could find me working hard on my latest big-bucks case. Eventually I would have hired an assistant, someone to answer the phone and do filing. Someone who didn't bother me with crap I didn't want to know. Maybe a twenty-something hunk with very little body hair and a six-pack.

The reality for me was this: many of my clients didn't want to come to an office. They preferred dealing with their clandestine business in coffee shops, where meetings could be spun as a harmless visit and a cup of coffee with me, a dear friend. I couldn't really blame them; I valued my privacy too. Of course, this was Merope, population twenty thousand or so, and privacy was a commodity hard to come by.

Their discretion was an illusion anyway. Everyone on the island knew what I did for a living.

The rest of my clients lived off the island and we did all our business via email, phone, and Skype. They didn't care if Finders Keepers had an office or not, as long as I could locate whatever their hearts and heads desired.

I flipped through the scant local paper and sipped my rapidly-cooling coffee. Kyria Olga's murder was already head-line news. The article was accompanied by an old picture, snapped long before the lilac hair and liver spots. I sat there for a time, rolling the paper cup between my hands, trying to make the hurt subside.

A group of teenage girls sat giggling around the corner table. They were having a blast pointing at customers and poking fun at everyone coming through the door. They could get away with it. They were dead, and had been since their car had a head-on collision with a semi-trailer hauling manure a year ago on the mainland. I made eye contact with one of the girls and raised an eyebrow. She whispered to her friends, and they settled down. I heard one of them sniping about how they couldn't even escape grown-ups in the afterlife.

When only the dregs remained in my cup, I shoved it through the swinging mouth of the trash can.

"Allie?"

I looked up into a vaguely familiar face. Brown hair slightly disheveled like he'd just finished rolling around in the hay. Tall. Nice build with broad shoulders. Hazel eyes. He was hot. He was gorgeous. He was—

"Allie Callas? Leo Samaras ... Detective Leo Samaras. I figured after last night we were on first name basis." His eyes twinkled. There was a smile in them that wasn't on his lips. "You said no to my roofies, so I gave you an aspirin instead."

The hot cop.

Where was a rock when I needed a hiding place?

"The Olga Marouli murder," he prompted. I craned my neck to look up at him. He was so much taller than me.

"I know who you are," I said, trying not to act like a total moron. "You just have fewer eyes than I remember, plus, you look nothing like the Elephant Man."

The grim line of his mouth twitched a little. At least he was polite enough not to laugh in my face. Big brownie points right there. "Business or pleasure?" he asked.

"Business. And now I have to take care of some more business."

Not really a lie, that was such an ugly word, more like ... fabrication.

He stood still, blocking the doorway. "What do you do?"

"I'm run my own business. Finders Keepers."

"The local snoop?"

He'd heard of me. Was that good or bad? I watched his face, trying to decide.

"That's a small part of it. Mostly I find weird stuff for old ladies."

The detective nodded thoughtfully. "Is that right? Then you know the protocol. I'll be by this evening. I still have some questions for you."

"I thought I knew all the cops on the island."

His smile was tight. "I'm a local, just been out of town a long time. Got a transfer back from Thessaloniki last month." He stepped aside, leaving the path clear for me to leave.

So I did. Then I stopped.

My grandmother's pearls of wisdom popped into my head. *A lady always remembers her manners ... unless she forgets them on purpose.* Unfortunately, they were followed by more of her words such as: *Never hit a man unless he is holding a paddle and begging for a spanking; Never trust a man with a pulse;* and, *A lady never spits unless it is in someone's face and they deserve it.* If some people are salt of the earth, my grandmother was the dirt.

A split second before the glass door closed, I stopped it. "Detective Samaras?"

"Yes?"

"Thanks. The aspirin really helped."

His mouth turned up at the edges. "Any time."

The feeling of familiarity swept over me followed by the tickle of dry mouth. I uncurled my fingers from the door handle and let it fall into place. I shivered despite the warm fall day. It was the same feeling I got sometimes when I walked past the cemetery.

I hurried back to my bicycle quickly. The October sun and my fast pace did their best to shake the anxiety out of my bones. It lingered until I flung my leg over the bar and shut the world out. I adjusted my cross-body bag and went to push away from the ragged sidewalk.

Out of nowhere a ball of light appeared. It jiggled, bounced, and dropped into my bicycle's basket. The ball slowly expanded until the light faded and Kyria Olga was in its place, spilling over the edges of the basket.

This was freaky, even for me. Usually ghosts are just ghosts. Regular people, except see-through.

"Stop scaring the *kaka* out of me, please?" I asked, a hint of desperation creeping into my voice.

She clapped her hands and laughed. "Do you like my new trick? We learned that one at orientation. It is so much fun to be a ball of light! I can do different colors too. Pick a color."

I cast a rueful eye at my basket, which was visible all the way up to her diaphragm. The bars stuck out of her ribcage. "Can you not get any ectoplasm on my basket, please?"

Her ghostly hand waved, dismissing me. "Eh ... we do not learn to make ectoplasm for another three semesters. Apparently it can be quite dangerous to attempt it before you are ready. Something about turning your own limbs into goo."

"Well, that's a relief," I said. "Do you suppose you could warn me before you start to ooze all over my things?"

She heaved a sigh, more dramatic in death than she had been in life. "I suppose those worthless children of mine will descend upon my apartment like a pack of vultures soon. They will grab everything they can get their sticky, fat fingers on."

I didn't doubt it. Kyria Olga had three children, and they all suffered from terminal selfishness, never coming to Merope to see their mother unless there was something in it for them. I'd made a point never to visit when they were around.

Her words triggered something. "That reminds me.

Kyrios Psaris came by earlier. He looked heartbroken, so you might swing by and watch over him for a while."

"Dear Stavros ..." She glared at me. "Are you trying to get ride of me?"

"Me? No. He's in love with you, you know."

She tipped back her head. Laughter burbled out. "In love with me? Where do you get these things, my doll? Stavros is not in love with me."

"Is too."

"Still snippy I see." Her arms folded, and she turned to stare at the sea while I peddled. The sea was its usual autumn self, wearing dishwater gray instead of its summer outfit of blues and greens. It lapped at the boats tethered to the dock. My friend was dead but the world kept quietly turning.

We rode in silence, Olga playing passenger, me crawling along Main Street slightly faster than a snail. When I turned off the busiest street in town, a sign caught my eye. There was a new shop on the island and I hadn't even heard about it. I suffer from chronic sweet tooth at the best of times, but suddenly the bottom dropped out of my blood sugar levels and an instant craving for something gooey and sweet galloped through me. The sign above the door read, in English, *Cake Emporium*, then underneath in smaller old English style type, *Your one-stop shop for sugary treats*.

Count me in.

"What are you doing?"

"Buying cake?"

"What about my murder?"

"I can't solve a murder without cake in my belly."

Kyria Olga's lips formed a tight disapproving pucker. She glared at me for a moment then said, "If you are going to be such a *kolopetha,* I am leaving."

"Fine!" I didn't want to be around anyone who called me a butt-child anyway.

With the soft pop of a bursting soap bubble she blinked out of sight.

The Cake Emporium was definitely new. I was practically a spaniel when it came to sniffing out sweets. Not that I indulged all the time. I tried to keep it down to a piece or twelve per day, with extra—a lot extra—on the days I did an excess of bike riding.

For a moment, my brain stuttered. The window display looked nothing like any bakery I'd ever seen before. A midnight blue curtain served as a backdrop for the elaborate display. A crystal ball cake sat atop a cloth-draped table. Marzipan knick knacks filled the shelves of knee-high book-case, and a slab of Ouija board cake with letters in chocolate frosting and a spun sugar pointer told me that this wasn't just any old cake shop that sold lemon meringue pie and cupcakes.

I tried not to leave a nose print on the sparkling glass as I flattened it this way and that, trying to get a peek past the curtain. It was no good; the curtain blocked off all view of the store contents. For all I knew the proprietors were inside sacrificing a cheesecake goat on a black forest altar.

The door was a natural progression of the window display; stars, the moon, and a pair of sprites dancing under the moonshine around what looked like a cherry pie.

I chained my bicycle to the nearby rack, pocketed the key and went to investigate. Normally I didn't bother with the chain, but I was probably going to be inside a while and wouldn't be able to see the street with that curtain in the way.

A blanket of warmth slipped over me as I stepped inside. The air inside was a delicious concoction of strawberries and chocolate with a dash of vanilla. I could curl up in a ball and live here forever.

Whatever I'd expected, it wasn't this cornucopia of gastronomical delights. Two cabinets--one refrigerated and one not-contained dozens of tiny cakes. Little iced bats, bright orange pumpkin cupcakes, all of my favorite things. The walls were covered in every piece of occult and Halloween paraphernalia possible. All of it, I suspected, was edible. Pots and jars of all kinds of baking ingredients sat on shelves, waiting to be plucked up by an eager amateur baker.

If one side held sugary tributes to occult, the other side held the real thing in a perfect mirror image. Real tarot cards, real jars with the unidentifiable concealed within. Light and dark, something for each side.

Black spots danced in front of my eyes as the pupils adjusted to the dim light. The only light source other than the cabinets was coming from the candles atop each of four tiny tables. I wondered how the Merope Fire Department felt about the fire risk.

"Don't worry, they're electric," a girlish voice said from behind the counter.

I leaned over the polished counter and peered past the antique cash register. A woman of uncertain age, draped in a royal purple caftan, smiled at me from an overstuffed armchair. A plate of strawberries and cream balanced precariously on her knees.

"Excuse me?"

"The candles. That's what you were wondering—yes?" She stared at me from behind large, round glasses that had last been popular during the eighties. I still couldn't pin an age to her. With skin that smooth she should be a teenager, but her eyes said she'd been around since the dinosaurs died screaming in a meteor collision.

"No ... yes ... huh?"

"Oh, don't worry, I don't read minds all the time. Although I do know why you've come to us." Setting the strawberries aside, the woman stood up and took my hand across the counter. It was tiny against mine. "I'm Betty. Betty Honeychurch."

"You're not—"

"Greek?"

"Yes."

"We're English."

"Allie Callas. How do you—"

"A gift. We've both been smart enough to turn our gifts into good fortune, haven't we?" She positively beamed at me. I found it soothing, despite the zillion questions forming in my head.

"Who is 'we'?"

"This store belongs to my brother and me. Do you like our little shop?"

I didn't really know how to answer. "I'm surprised there's a viable market for this kind of stuff in Merope. I mean, the cakes I get but people here have been steeped in religion since birth. They believe in some woo-woo things, but only the woo-woo things that have been handed down through the generations. They're not really open to new woo-woo things."

Betty laughed. "Oh, people here are no different from any place else. Everybody wants to peek into the future or make someone love them, so they come here. They get a little help and leave with a cookie to sweeten the deal."

"And you give them what they're looking for?"

"That is up to them. I can't seem to get it through their thick skulls that free will is the wild card of divination. Most people pick out the parts they want to hear and believe and then they discard the rest. But back they come the next time they want to see the path ahead." She shook her head slightly. Tightly permed curls jiggled and bobbled about her head. As she wrapped up her spiel, she grasped my hand again and pulled me across the room to one of the three tables. "Come on," she said. "Let's talk about what brought you here."

"You mean sugar?"

"I can't see every thought," she said. "It's more like flashes and blips. But I can see why you're here. I'd just like to hear it from your own lips. That would only be polite, seeing how you're one of us."

"Us?" I was starting to repeat myself.

She leaned forward and whispered, "The gifted."

"But I'm not--"

"Of course you are. You've been living with it quietly for most of your life."

I leaned back in the chair and stared at the wall. A Balinese dance mask mocked me, its huge Mick Jagger-esque lips curved in a perpetually cheesy grin.

"How can you tell?"

Betty offered the plate of strawberries. I took one and bit into the red flesh. It was sweet with barely a hint of tartness. Uncommon for this time of year when summer had already dribbled out the door.

"It's your aura. All of us who have gifts have a little extra zing to our auras. Although you've got a sprinkling of black around your shoulders right now. Overwhelming responsibility ... stress ... sadness ... pain? You were a friend of the murdered woman?"

"Yes," I murmured. If I thought about it too hard the tears would start to cascade down my cheeks again.

"But?"

"But she's ... You won't think I'm a complete lunatic?"

Betty shook her head. Sausage curls slapped her cherubic cheeks.

I took a deep breath and went for it. "Kyria Olga is haunting me. She expects me to find her killer."

"And what form did she take? Some intangible form? A mist perhaps?"

"She looks the same as she did before she ... before she died. Right down to the widows' weeds and beehive 'do."

"Ah." Her fingers formed a steeple and she twiddled her thumbs. "Seeing spirits. A useful gift—and quite uncommon with your level of skill."

My fingers dripped with red berry juice. Betty slid a linen napkin to me and went back to twiddling.

"Useful?"

"The dead can be quite helpful at times. But if they figure out that you can do more than see them ... You might discover they become quite persistent."

"They already know."

She chuckled. "You're lucky you don't have the dead from here to Timbuktu—good heavens, is there even such a place? —begging you to help them."

"You mean besides Kyria Olga?"

"Look at it this way, your friend has all the time in the world now to make sure you do, whether it is practical or not. I can tell you this though, you need to be careful. Someone wishes you harm."

"Olga's killer?"

"No. But I can see that someone is about to be very unhappy with you."

"Just my luck," I said.

"Now," she said, leaning forward. Even in the dim light a twinkle danced in her eyes. "Tell me about this policeman you met last night ..."

CHAPTER FIVE

Four strawberry fingers, six pumpkin cupcakes, and a bag of marzipan skulls later, I returned to the outside world, dazed. For a moment, darks spots blinded me. I pulled my bag open and dug deep for my sunglasses.

Why did I have to commune with the dead? Why couldn't I have a useful gift, like, say, being able to reach into my handbag and immediately find the object I needed? But no-o-o-o I wasn't that lucky.

My sunglasses were nestled at the bottom, between a lip balm and an old tissue. Wiping the worst of the lint away, I balanced them on my nose and waited. The spots faded and my bicycle swam into focus. All I needed was the key to unlock the chain, but my fingers couldn't find it. I peered into my bag, then a small noise jerked my head up.

I froze.

There was a figure standing by my bicycle. Well, more like leaning. Not a ghost. Not unless ghosts were completely solid and dressed in black from head to toe. I couldn't see his face but he was positively exuding cool. His hair was as dark as his clothing and curled at the point where neck met collar. Long coat. Boots. He reminded me of a refugee from one of Jane Austen's novels: all mood and fog and pride.

Except for the shadows slanted across most of his face. Now that was weird, especially on a sunny morning.

I shook my head and brushed the romantic whimsy aside.

All that black, maybe he was some kind of angel of doom. That would be about right.

He was holding something out in his hand. I glanced from side to side then back again at the figure and did a *Who, me?* shrug.

"Yes, you."

His voice was deep, melodic, hypnotic. It conjured up images of old libraries, and crackling fireplaces, and maps covered in strange, fantastical lands.

I slid my hand into my purse and curled my fingers around the pepper spray I kept for emergencies like this.

Like this? Who was I kidding? Nothing else had even been quite like this.

"Are you lost?" I asked.

"No. Not lost."

Last of the great verbal communicators right here in Merope, folks.

"Do you need help? Because the police station is right down ..." I pointed east-ish.

He shook his head and held out his hand. That's how I really knew he wasn't from Greece. Greeks show their negatives with a chin tilt, up then down. But his words were Greek, with a dusting of another tongue.

Finally I was close enough to get a close-up look at this guy. He wasn't as tall as I first thought, maybe just a touch under six-feet. The broad shoulders, tapering down into muscular arms and a narrow waist just made him seem larger than he was. Nope, definitely not a ghost. Even under the black shirt and pants I could see he was a guy who took care of himself. Not a runner or a diaper-wearing steroids freak, but someone who did some type of manual labor every day.

"You're not much of a talker are you? Is this going to turn into one of those charades things, because I'm going to tell you right now, I really suck at charades."

His hand darted out and grabbed mine--the one that wasn't purse-deep and gripping pepper spray.

"Hey! Help!" I pulled my hand from my purse. The spray bottle caught on the lip and landed on the asphalt with a dull clank. I was so screwed. My eyes locked with the stranger's as I prepared my please-don't-hurt-me-oh-crazy-but-merciful-lunatic speech.

He released my hand. Surprised, I pulled away. There was something in my hand, something shiny.

"Hey, my key!" I looked up into a pair of deep, dark eyes framed with thick dark lashes.

He nodded, his dark eyes holding mine.

I broke away first, crouching down to unlock the chain.

"Where did you find it?"

Silence.

I looked up. He was gone.

Funny, I would have sworn he was alive.

———

Kyrios Yiannis, the apartment building's long-dead former gardener, was knee-deep in gardenias and bougainvillea in the small yard. I stopped peddling and watched for a moment. This was as close as I'd even get to gardening. When it came to plants I had the black thumb of death. When I first moved into my apartment, my mother and Toula bought ferns as housewarmings gifts. One died within a month; the other dragged its terminal illness out to six months. Finally I just tossed it in the trash and put an end to its misery. Botanical euthanasia. After that no one gave me plants.

Kyrios Yiannis waved a gloved hand, and I waved back discretely, thinking if someone saw me I could pretend I was scratching my nose, or picking my teeth.

The sweet scent of sugary treats wafted up from the cardboard box nestled inside the blue and gold Cake Emporium bag. I wiggled my finger inside and scooped out a finger-load of orange frosting.

Licking at my finger like a hungry dog, I traipsed upstairs, forgoing the elevator for the stairs. I figured the stairs were good for at least a cupcake. By the time my feet hit the top step, I was down to three cupcakes. And there was worse news waiting just down the hall.

Slouched against my door, looking like he had all the time in the world to hang out and sip coffee, Detective Samaras flipped a palm up at me. Not the full five-fingered, open-palmed *moutsa* that meant he thought I had a chronic masturbation issue, but a real wave. I flipped a feeble wave back.

Great.

Not that I had anything to hide, but ... why me? It was too late to sneak back down the stairs; he'd already spotted me. So I forged on ahead, putting on my best cool, calm, and collected expression that I'd perfected in front of the bathroom mirror when I was thirteen. A stoic face was a necessity when a dead teenager from a bygone era hopped around your math class and humped the teacher's leg.

"Are you here for this evening's show? Because by my watch you're early." I rubbed discretely at my mouth, hoping I didn't have frosting and crumbs stuck to my face.

It was marching toward late morning and the sun had shifted. leaving the hallway in shadows. Despite the lack of light, I could tell he wasn't smiling. He tipped the cup and swallowed as I neared.

"I figured you'd show sooner or later. I still have questions."

"Why detective, you're practically a stalker." I unlocked the door and ushered him in.

"Nice place," he said, staring out of the window at my view of the parking lot. "Looks just like mine."

"Huh?" Great. The pearls just kept on coming today. At this rate he was going to throw me in a cell, guilty of chronic stupidity.

He hooked a thumb at the ceiling. "We're neighbors, remember?"

It slowly came back to me. He was the neighbor with the revolving door sex life.

"You could say I'm on top," he went on.

It made me snippy. I wanted to slap myself around the face but instead took it out on the cop. "Or ... you could do your job and ask your questions."

What was it about this guy that had my hackles raised? Was it that he had seen me at my most vulnerable, completely smashed and I barely remembered it?

His face shifted back to its stony tough-cop veneer. Without emotion he took the armchair. I maintained my distance and sat on the sofa, the coffee table forming a barrier between us.

He pulled the notepad from his jacket pocket. Déjà vu. "How well did you know Olga Marouli?"

"We were neighbors and friends."

"Are a lot of your friends older?"

"Than what?" I snapped.

"Than you."

"I have very few friends and too many acquaintances."

"Why?"

"Mostly I'm comfortable with my own company. A closet introvert."

"What time did you enter Olga Marouli's apartment?"

"About 6:oo P.M."

"Her front door was open?"

"Not wide. The door was ajar, about a few centimeters or so."

"Where were you between five and six?"

It was his job to ask questions, but it still bugged me. I stood and stalked into the kitchen where my trash can was overflowing. I found what I was looking for easily. The receipt from the supermarket indicated that I'd paid for my things at 5:42 P.M. Next stop was the printer, where the left-over time-stamped photographs of the Dimitri and Maria lay in the tray.

With a flick of the wrist, I dropped everything in his lap. "Have fun."

His eyes focused immediately on what he needed to see. "I wouldn't normally say this, but, you're off the hook. I didn't think you were good for it anyway."

"Good. I'll sleep better tonight," I snapped.

He ignored my bitchy tone. "Just one more thing. Can you think of anyone who might have wanted Olga Marouli dead?"

I thought for a moment and came up empty. "No. She wasn't wealthy, and she was always kind. I can't imagine why she was targeted."

"She have any regular visitors?"

"Besides me? Sure. But I didn't exactly run to the peep-hole every time someone rang her doorbell."

"Can't you throw at least one name at me?"

"Stavros Psaris, her late husband's best friend. They ate together at least once a week."

"What about family?"

A massive hog-like snort made my nostrils sting. "I've never met them but they'd show up occasionally from the mainland when they wanted something."

"Like money?"

"I don't know, I wasn't privy to the conversation."

"Are you seeing anybody?"

"Just the dead," I muttered.

He paused and looked up from the notebook. "That's not what I meant."

My cheeks flushed.

Slowly, deliberately, he flipped the notebook cover and slipped it back into his pocket. "Thanks for your time. If I have any more questions ..."

"You'll be back?"

"Yes." The cop mask slipped for a moment, leaving a smile in its place. It made me want to see more. Just as quickly, it vanished. "We're done with the crime scene if you want to take a look around. As her friend, you might see something we missed. So long as you don't mind if I tag along."

"No problem." I nodded, grateful for his offer. I had contemplated taking a look around Olga's apartment on my own, but picking the lock didn't seem polite. Or legal. Detective Samaras indicated that he'd be back in a moment. He disappeared down the hall, returning two minutes later, keys in hand.

"I have Kyria Olga's keys," he said and swung the door to apartment 201 wide open.

We stepped inside. A chill gyrated deep inside my bones. The apartment was exactly as it had always been. Nothing was different except that my friend was longer here to greet me.

Tears pricked my eyes. "Is it okay if I touch anything?"

"We already took fingerprints, so yes."

I ran a hand lovingly across the rocking chair Olga favored. We spent many evenings chatting about this and that while her knitting needles clicked, her heels rising and falling as she rocked slowly in the chair. I often found myself lulled by the rhythmic motion. It was homey and made me wish my own Grandmother had owned such a chair. My grandmother had one of those leather vibrating chairs. And no, she didn't have arthritis.

The knitting bag occupied its usual place, filled with needles and wool in a dozen different colors. I recognized the bright red wool she'd been working with most recently. The pattern, an afghan with a Christmas motif, lay spread out on the spindle legged coffee table. She'd never have the chance to finish the piece. Not now.

A single tear spilled over the rim of my eye. It rolled down my cheek then paused when it hit my chin. My bottom lip quivered and the single tear was joined by a dozen more.

I'm not a crier.

The last time I'd indulged a really good weep-fest was when ten-year-old me broke my arm falling out of a tree. When my sister made fun of me for crying over my broken bone, the tears dried up and my fist connected with her nose. My parents had to carry two children into the emergency room that night. Toula was still bitter.

Even when Miles deserted me, I'd squelched the sobbing and opted for severe tearless depression instead. I kept that up for a month and then hurled myself back into work.

Blinking back the tears, I refocused. It didn't do me any good to dwell on that night in the Super Super Market. The past was past and there it had to stay, locked up tight, compartmentalized, and unable to do me harm.

Instead of scoffing, Detective Samaras touched my shoulder. "I'm sorry for your loss," he said. I didn't need to look up to see he was sincere.

"S'okay," I said, sniffing.

"Can I get you some more aspirin?"

I gave a half snort, half laugh, and a big bubble of saliva

ballooned out of my mouth. My hand slapped my mouth, but it was too late. He'd spotted it. Who could miss it? All I needed now were snot bubbles. Those really get a guy hot.

"It's alive," he said.

This time there was no mistaking his smile. Straight white teeth, nice lips, a very attractive smile.

The second snort burst out before I could stop it. The bubble popped, leaving spit on my chin. My cheeks flushed.

"I'm a pig. A human pig."

Detective Samaras shook his head and laughed. He pulled a tissue from his pocket and wiped my chin. I guess he dealt with snotty women with over-active salivary glands on a daily basis. His hand found its way back to my shoulder. No doubt, the first time his intention was to comfort me. This time around it created a line of heat that started at my shoulder and burned a trail south. His close proximity made me hyper-aware; the faintest touch of cologne, or perhaps body wash, tickled my nostrils. The fragrance smelled fresh, with a slight tang of citrus.

He was close. Too close for my antisocial comfort. Which meant that I noticed things that I hadn't noticed earlier. My eyes fastened on his mouth. Why hadn't I noticed his lips sooner? The bottom was slightly fuller than the top with a slight natural upturn at the edges. The cop in him must battle hard to keep a smile at bay.

Would he cuff me if I reached up and bit his bottom lip?

Stop it! my inner voice yelped.

This is what happened when I went without sex for a while. I ended up in some dirty fantasy with someone completely inappropriate, like Detective Samaras. With all the action he had going on upstairs, it wasn't difficult to stretch my imagination as far as his bed. Or his kitchen. Or his floor. Or this floor. Or any floor.

I looked away first, not wanting to be mistaken for a

desperate lunatic. His opinion of me as a drunk was already formed; I had no intention of adding nympho to it.

Eager to put some distance between us, I tentatively checked out the kitchen where I'd found my friend.

"Anything missing?" he asked.

I took my time, meticulously reconciling the décor now with what it had been just twenty-four hours earlier. Everything was the same. Even the dozens of fridge magnets Kyria Olga collected were still displayed on her refrigerator; everything from miniature gardens to cutesy sayings. My favorite was one I'd given her that read, *Who left the bag of idiots open?*

"No," I said. "It looks like it always did. I take it you did an inventory of her jewelry, the pieces she was wearing when ..."

He pulled the notebook out of pocket again and flipped to the first page. "One plain gold band and marquise diamond on the left. An emerald cut sapphire on the right hand, middle finger. Small gold cross around her neck and two gold studs, one in each ear, some type of knot design."

I nodded. "That sounds right. Those were the pieces she usually wore. French knots."

"That must be some sort of woman lingo."

"French knots are a particular type of knot. You wrap the thread around the needle before pulling it through fabric."

"So you're domesticated too?" His tone was smile-tinted.

"I'm a good Greek girl, I can hold my own. So my guess is this wasn't a burglary gone wrong."

He flipped through the pages of his notebook again and scribbled. I craned my neck slightly trying to score a glance at his notes. He rewarded me by slamming it shut. Spoilsport.

"I agree with you," he said evenly

I thought about Kyria Olga's request. Was this a crime of passion, convenience, or kicks? I wondered how much of the investigation the detective was willing to share. Would it hurt to ask? Worst case he'd say nothing. Best case he'd tell me something that might appease my friend.

"Do you have a list of suspects yet?"

"Nothing concrete. We lifted some prints but no matches, except for yours. I might have a clearer picture when we pull her financials and start figuring out who had something to gain by her death."

It was no surprise that my prints were in the database. I'd spent a night in the lockup after Miles left and I went on a bender that ended with me sleeping on a haystack, surrounded by goats.

Suddenly, the front door opened with so much force it bounced off the wall behind it. We both jumped back. The detective instinctively reached for his gun.

"Do not even think about taking a single thing. Not unless you have a warrant. I know how these things work. I watch those police shows—*all* the police shows."

The voice belonged to a lump of pallid pizza dough. Lank blah-colored hair hung around a moon face. She added a dose of color to the subtle apartment with her fuchsia and turquoise polyester separates. Her clothing didn't clash; it waged bitter war. I recognized her from the photos of her younger self that hung on these very walls; Olga Marouli's eldest daughter. And she wasn't alone.

CHAPTER SIX

The whole motley gang had arrived, each of them eager to grab a piece of the possession pie. My eyes slid to an old family snapshot of the Marouli family hanging on the wall and super-imposed it over the group standing in the entranceway.

The visual night terror in Polynesian polyester was Athena, Kyria Olga's eldest child. Hovering behind her like a shaky Chihuahua, Marko, Athena's long suffering husband, avoided all eye contact. Marko could be summed up in one insignificant word: beige. *Athena made a change purse out of his scrotum years ago*, Kyria Olga told me one night over a couple of glasses of sweet *mavrodaphne* wine. Looking at him now, I didn't doubt it. His hand hovered around his groin, probably looking for his missing goobers.

Tina Marouli, middle child and divorcee, took up half the space of her older sister. Mid-forties, she was a woman who took care of herself with regular trips to the salon to keep her sandy hair streaked and her nails perfect. Her nose bore that slight sharpness that comes from a surgeon's knife. The edges of her mouth sagged. Her eyes had a chemical glaze.

I knew from my talks with Kyria Olga that Tina had one daughter, Lydia, and spoiled her to a fault without giving much in the way of affection. Lydia was a wild girl who'd recently been arrested for soliciting an undercover policeman. She was nowhere in sight.

The baby of the family was George Marouli. He shared watery eyes with his eldest sister, and what little was left of his hair was also the same dull shade of dirty blond. His build was slight. His belly said he was well on his way to his third trimester. Accompanying him, his two boys. His wife left six months earlier, deserting her husband for another woman; George's secretary, if memory served. Judging from the looks he was shooting at my insignificant rack, he was ready to leap back on to the bucking bronco.

Fat chance, cowboy.

His two boys were best described as sulky. Teenagers. The oldest of the two was sliding his gaze appraisingly all over Detective Samaras. The younger boy was the lovechild of Marilyn Manson and the Wicked Witch of the West. His spiked hair was dipped in black and the requisite safety pin threaded through his bottom lip. Charming. He was the only one in black. Nobody else had dressed for mourning, a major faux-pas when a Greek family member dies. It's supposed to be a year-long commitment, at least.

"You're related to the deceased?" Detective Samaras addressed Athena, who was making the most fuss. He was all business; I couldn't read him, couldn't grasp his impression of the Marouli gang.

"Related!" Athena made a clucking sound. "We are her babies!" A meaty hand clutched at her chest, twisting the polyester to breaking point. Fat tears dripped off her chin. They met their sticky end in her voluminous cleavage. Marko shuffled his feet, offering no comfort to his wife. He probably resented being neutered.

The detective took a step forward. "Detective Samaras. I'm in charge of this investigation.

Athena's watery eyes slid over to me. "Who are you? You don't look much like a cop."

"Allie Callas. I live across the hall. You mother and I were neighbors. May her memory be eternal."

She ignored my traditional greeting. "Of course you were neighbors if you lived across the hall."

George stepped forward. "Don't be so rude, Athena." We shook hands and he introduced himself. "If you need insurance, I'm your man." His chest puffed up. "These are my sons, Stathis and Tomas."

"Tomas, are you gothic?" I asked the younger boy.

The boy rolled his black kohl rimmed eyes. "Eww no. I'm an emo."

I was much too old for this and seriously out of touch with the current youth movement. "Like *Tickle Me Emo?*"

His eyes rolled even further this time. I'd swear I saw his optic nerve bundle. "An emo is like a Goth, but depressed."

"Got it. An emo is a Goth on Prozac."

No one laughed except his father. A cacophony erupted from George's mouth. He sounded like a goose on *sisa* —Greece's meth.

The rational part of me wanted to run like hell and hide in the safe confines of my own apartment, away from the scary people. The nosy part wanted to stay. Morbid curiosity might have killed the cat but it was my bread and butter. I decided to stay, just to see how the detective handled the Marouli clan.

I glanced sideways at the detective. His jaw was iron, pulsing periodically. Was it my imagination or was he starting to look uncomfortable? From what I knew of the Maroulis they could drive the Dalai Lama to drugs and debauchery.

Athena pushed her way past us into the living room. Her

beady eyes scanned the room. "You better not have taken anything."

"None of your mother's possessions were collected," Detective Samaras said.

"Who did it?" Athena asked.

"We're following some leads."

Athena's head snapped around. "Are you telling me you don't know who killed my beloved mother?"

"It's under investigation. Your mother's murder has my full attention."

"Is that a yes or a no? I want an answer." She stamped her foot. Everyone around her remained shell-shocked.

Detective Samaras stayed steady. "I can't give out details of an ongoing investigation."

"Well, you better go do your job then. I do not pay taxes so you can just sit around, counting your *archidia*."

Balls. She meant balls.

Athena dropped into the rocking chair I'd lovingly touched a few minutes earlier. The wood creaked. "Marko, George, get our luggage. No reason to pay for a hotel when Mama is not using her apartment anymore."

I sucked in my cheeks, trying to force the expression of horror away. Detective Samaras glanced over at me; he was starting to look haunted.

He pulled a business card from his pocket. "This is my contact information if you have any questions."

Probably he would live to regret those words.

Athena flicked the card on to the coffee table. "Since you are leaving, do you know the number for a good delivery food around here? We're in mourning. We can't go out."

Greek families in mourning don't socialize. It's serious taboo to court fun during the first forty days. As previously mentioned, Greek families in mourning also wear black. This bunch, apart from the youngest boy, looked like a circus. So their dedication wasn't exactly all-encompassing.

Across the chair, the detective's eyes met mine. I knew what he was going to say next.

"Yes, Kyria Athena, you might try Crusty Dimitri's." He rattled off the number all residents of Merope know by heart ... even though the sane ones never eat there when they're sober.

"George, call them," Athena barked.

"Why me? You call."

"My mother just died. Too much grief."

"She was my mother, too."

"It is different for daughters," Athena said.

The detective's lips pressed together until they formed a tight white line. I knew what he was suppressing; I felt it burbling up inside me too.

I left in a hurry

"Wait for me," the detective said.

I threw my front door open and we collapsed, laughing until our bellies ached and tears poured down our faces.

————

Crusty Dimitri's serves gyro and souvlaki with a side of acid reflux. And that's before you even take a bite of the food. The store, which is really more like a shack, is located off the main street, two doors down from the Merope Courthouse. Décor includes two wobbly tables, five shaky chairs and Medusa's head on the wall opposite the front door. Dimitri's patrons are late risers, heavy drinkers, and the unsuspecting tourists who pass by on the way to Merope's museum. It's famous for serving bugs on the side the same way most *tavernas* throw in chunk of bread or two. The meat is a mystery, but I've heard a lot of disembodied meowing in the area. In most cities, the health inspector would have forced Crusty Dimitri's to shape up or close its doors, but, in an odd twist of fate, Crusty Dimitr's brother is the health inspector. So the bugs stay put and the cats stay away—far away.

The Maroulis deserved it.

"I can't believe you recommended Crusty Dimitri's," I managed to say through the laughter.

"They were asking for it."

I wrapped my arms around my stomach. "Who knew you had a sense of humor, Detective Samaras."

"Leo."

"Leo."

We held the gaze for a moment too long. I broke away first, fixing my eyes to a spot on the wall, where a sphere of light had appeared above him. It was dancing on his head.

Kyria Olga was back.

I watched half-horrified while the ball zigzagged around him. Detective Samaras—Leo—was oblivious. I had to get rid of him. Fast.

"I guess you better get back to work then," I said quickly, trying not to focus on the bouncing light.

"Something wrong?"

The ball of light zoomed between his legs and hovered on his crotch.

I flinched. My throat clamped shut, leaving my voice to squeak out, "No, of course not."

"You're a strange woman."

"You have no idea."

His mouth lifted into a stiff smile. He obviously thought I was throwing him out, which was pretty much true.

"You know where to find me if you hear anything worth passing along."

I formed a pistol with the fingers of one hand. "You bet."

With mixed emotions, I pushed the door shut behind

him. He'd handled the Maroulis like the pro he was. But even more, he surprised me with a wicked display of humor. I hadn't expected that. In truth I like putting people in boxes, figuring out what makes up their psyche. It's rare that anyone surprises me. And right now I was surprised. Big time.

With a small sigh, I turned back to the bobbing light.

"You can come out now."

"I think I will stay like this," Kyria Olga said. "It is very liberating. No body to weigh me down."

"Suit yourself," I said dryly.

She followed me into the kitchen, hovering above the countertop while I poured a glass of water.

"I see the vultures have landed."

Had they ever. They were busy pecking at the bones already. "Hard to believe they're yours."

"They used to be such loving children. Now ... they are almost strangers."

"They're something all right. That grandson of yours better not get too close to all those magnets on the fridge." I took a small sip of the water. "I wonder if one of them killed you."

A sigh escaped the golden ball. "My own family! *Gamo tin Panayia mou*, what are you thinking?"

Kyria Olga's mouth was considerably saltier since her untimely death.

"It happens all the time."

"Not in my family!"

"Fine, but the list of suspects is slim. Nothing was stolen, and ..." I tapped a finger on my chin, "... you weren't having an affair—wait, were you?"

"I most certainly was not!" Her voice climbed several decibels. The ball of light flickered.

"Well, that leaves random gratuitous killing, unless you

drove someone to murder." I narrowed my eyes. "Kyria Olga, did you give someone a *moutsa*?"

Though she wasn't in human form, I could almost see her lips pursing. "I did no such thing. A woman of good character never—"

My cellphone buzzed.

Toula.

"What's wrong?" My words scrambled out, frantic and fear-tinged. My sister never called unless it was to deliver bad news or question my life choices.

"Nothing. I just wanted to check on you."

"Well, I'm great, thanks for asking. You?"

"Fine." Toula wavered like she was waiting for me to make some fascinating conversation. She'd be waiting a while—I was all tapped out.

"Great," I said finally. "Have you heard from Mama and Baba?"

"No. You?"

"No. I haven't heard anything on the news about ships crashing into icebergs or succumbing to rogue waves, so I guess they're having a blast."

An icy freeze pierced my ear.

"Toula? Are you still there?"

"Why did you have to say that?"

"What?"

"Mama and Baba aren't going to die out there on that boat."

My eyes rolled back in my head. "It's a ship, and I never said they were."

Her voice became shrill. "It's bad luck to even mention it! There goes my sleep. Why do you always have to do this? Why are you so negative?"

Why me? I shook my head slowly, for my own benefit. "*Yiasou*, Toula. Call me sometime when you're capable of having a conversation with real adults."

"What's that supposed—"

End call.

Small doses. That's all I can handle of Toula and her frosty melodrama. It's downright impossible to have a joke with her without her flipping out. This was just more of the usual.

"That was not very nice, Allie. You are never mean."

"Oh great, now I'm being reprimanded by a ball of light that no one else can see. What next? Zombies?"

"There is no such thing as zombies."

"Good to know. That'll come in really handy next time I play a trivia game and get the zombie brain-eating question." I drained my water glass and stomped into the hallway, keys and bag in hand.

The ball of light trailed behind me. "Where are you going? You cannot just leave."

I kept walking. "It's Saturday," I said briskly. "I'm going to your knitting group."

"Do not forget to take a coat, eh? The weather could change at any moment."

———

Catty-corner to the Courthouse, the Merope Recreational Center is the hub for every sportsman, child, and club in Merope. The island's tax dollars are on display everywhere, from the low-tech basketball court to the lop-sided rose bushes and lone olive tree that form the Merope Botanical Gardens. Olga Marouli's knitting and crochet circle met every Saturday afternoon in the stone building.

I'd half expected Kyria Olga to follow me here, but when I cruised to a stop I was still alone. By all rights I was sticking my nose in police business. It was really Leo's place to be here, but the old ladies in Merope are a vicious bunch, prone to suspicion and always ready to thwart honest fact finding with dozens of gossipy stories about folks and families long gone—and the juicier and more sordid, the better. They take no prisoners and spare no one a good character assassination. It was definitely better for me to do this. Who knew what other tasty tidbit one of the ladies would accidentally drop?

I consoled myself by promising to turn over any information gleaned, no matter how insignificant; my intentions were completely honorable. All the same, my fingers stayed crossed as I pushed one of the two heavy doors open.

"Hey, you! Hold the door!"

I swiveled around and propped the door open with my back. My eyes scanned the air outside ... and dropped.

"What's your problem? Something look strange to you?"

The owner of the voice was a little person, about half my height. There were no little people on Merope, so he had to be a transplant or a temporary fixture.

I blinked. "No, should it?"

"I don't know, giant. You tell me."

Maybe he wasn't really a little person; maybe he was just weighed down by all his hair. God knows he had plenty of it, springing like blond wire out of his face and scalp. A bulging khaki messenger bag hung crosswise across his body, giving him a definite lean.

My eyes scanned the rectangular green name tag on his kiddy-sized polo shirt—also green. "Kontos?"

Was that a joke? I looked around, half expecting a camera crew to jump out. *Kontos* is one of the Greek words for *short*. It's also a legitimate last name, so I could only surmise that his family messed with the wrong Greek gods.

"Oh, so now there's something wrong with my name tag? Having a hard time reading it from all the way up there?"

"That's it. If I want any more lip out of you, I'll scrape it off my knee." I stepped forward and let the door swing shut. Through the glass panel, he shook his fist in rage.

"What's the matter? Can't you reach the handle?" I was officially the lowest of low, taunting a little person. Next I'd be tripping the elderly and kicking puppies.

"I can reach it just fine!"

I flicked the lock. "So open it then."

"*Gamisou*, you overgrown--"

I cupped my ear. "Sorry, I didn't quite catch that."

"Let. Me. In."

"Or what? You'll bite my kneecaps? Pinch my shins? Hump my leg?"

The little man spluttered. What I could see of his face was turning purple. "Just let me in."

"You want the giant to let you in?"

"Yes!"

"Will you give me three wishes if I do?"

"Three wi ... no! Do I look like a leprechaun? Has any one told you that you're a *strigla*?"

A witch. Charming.

"Funny, this particular *strigla* doesn't have to stretch to reach the handle." I turned away, but guilt gave me a jab. Being a big meanie doesn't come naturally to me. "Fine," I mumbled, and pushed the door open. The not-a-leprechaun glared at me. "It's not a trick," I told him.

"'Excuse me if I find you unreliable." His shoes made a soft pitter-patter as he hurried past me. "Giant cow," he muttered softly.

"What was that, *nanos*?"

Nanos is a less-than-flattering Greek term for a little person.

He whizzed around and pulled his leg back. I should have stepped back, but I didn't. How hard could half-pint kick, anyway?

Tears flooded my eyes as his sneaker connected with my ankle. I dropped to the floor and cradled my searing bones.

"That's what you get for making fun of me," Kontos said with a nasty little smirk.

I wanted blood, but it would have to wait. Right now I was too close to tears to give him a good, hard pinch.

"I'm going to kick your miniature ass," I said. Yeah, I sounded real convincing with that mewling whimper in my voice.

He walked away, middle finger raised. He might be half the size of most men but he was double the asshole.

I sat on the floor for several minutes, rubbing the owie. The painful patch beneath my jeans was quickly changing from red to purple. But the pain was all surface and the bone wasn't broken. The little twerp hadn't even broken the skin with his baby Reeboks.

Whatever. I was going to kick his ass anyway. If I recovered. With a groan, I propelled myself into a standing position and hobbled down the hall.

Kyria Olga's knitting class was down the corridor, left, then right. The frantic clicking of needle on needle as I approached the door told me I was going in the right direction.

Still hobbling, I pulled the door open and limped inside.

Marianna Papadopoulou, the youngest member of the group at sixty-something, served as leader and coordinator of all meetings and activities. I didn't really know her too well, and what little I did know was fairly benign. Kyria Olga used to refer to her as Little Mussolini. on account of how she ran the knitting group so tightly that it was nearly impossible for an outsider to join.

I snuck into the large airy room that was their meeting place and delivered the bad news about Olga Marouli's death to Kyria Marianna, just in case of the highly unlikely possibility that she didn't already know. I tactfully omitted the "m" word—murder— although the newspaper already apparently spelled out the grisly details in the weekend edition.

The news of Olga's murder knocked had Friday night's sports right off the front page. Murder was a rare beast around these parts and therefore automatically more sensational than sports—but only just.

"Poor Olga. I saw it in the newspaper and hoped there had been a mistake." Her thin lips quivered.

No, unfortunately there had been no mistake. The paper practiced accurate reporting, for once, although I hadn't yet read the article. The same family had been running Merope's newspaper since the town was founded. Nepotism was their standard, as was incest. The latest editor was one tiny step above imbecile.

"I wish it had been, Kyria Marianna. It's a horrible tragedy."

She patted my arm. "You poor thing, you found her, yes?"

Looks like the paper had spared few details. I made a noncommittal noise and changed the subject, "I was wondering if I might sit in on your group for a while. It might soothe me a little to chat to some of Kyria Marouli's friends."

She shrugged. "Of course, my doll. If it will make you feel better ..."

"It will," I assured her, lying through my teeth.

"Anything for a friend of Olga's." She turned to the group who were already busy chatting and knitting up a rainbow of yarn. "*Skasmos*! All that talking, you are giving me a headache. You all know Allie. She was Olga's friend and neighbor. And we all knew her grandmother, Kyria Foutoula."

Oh boy, she just had to bring that up.

"Kyria Foutoula—ha! She never met a *poutsa* she did not want to eat!"

The voice traveled from the back of the spacious room. Tough crowd.

Kyria Marianna tapped a finger on her temple. "Do not mind Vaso. She has lost her eggs and baskets." She turned back to the room. "Be nice to Allie. She is a good girl from a good family."

"Kyria Foutoula was a *putana*!" Kyria Vaso hollered. "A big one. Maybe the biggest one in history."

"A mostly good family," Kyria Marianna went on. "Make her feel like we want her here, okay, even if we do not." She turned back to me, her voice not even close to being suitable for indoors. "If they are rude to you, tell me and I will make them eat wood." She fixed a toothless smile on me.

Eating wood is a spanking, not an oral sex thing.

"One more question: where did Kyria Olga usually sit?"

Toothy smile still fixed on her face, she tugged on a springy chin hair. "Next to Kyria Kalliope. Over there."

I followed her finger.

Kalliope Kefala sat head down, needles flying. Her hair was bubblegum pink. What was with the hair? Something in Merope's water supply? Was I going to get an animalistic urge to dip my head in a vat of Easter egg dye on my seventieth birthday? I counted hair colors in faded orange, watered-down red, and pastel pink.

"Kyria Kalliope?"

The woman lifted her head. Her features were soft and unlined with high cheekbones. Her eyes were a watery caramel. A black cane with silver filigree accents lay at her side. Kyria Kalliope had been a great beauty in her time. There was a rumor that she'd wanted to compete in the Miss World competition, but her parents had slammed their Greek feet down, the way traditional Greek parents do, and forbidden her from competing.

"Kyria Kalliope," I said gently, "my name is Allie Callas. Kyria Olga was my friend."

The needles stopped and she patted the empty seat to her left. "Sit. Talk to me. I could use the company today."

She sat isolated from the others, not in distance, but in spirit. Other voices chattered around us, but Kyria Kalliope was alone. A pariah or just a loner? Kyria Olga didn't speak often of Kyria Kalliope, but I often had the feeling there was some point of contention between them. My friend and neighbor had never mentioned the basis of her prejudice, nor had she even admitted there was one. It was just a vague notion that struck me now and again. My own acquaintance with Kyria Kalliope was limited. I recalled sampling her *kataifi* (*bakalava's* hairier cousin) at a church festival a few years earlier. A steady stream of saliva flowed into my mouth as I recalled the burst of sweet and spicy. At the time I had complimented Kyria Kalliope on her recipe and she'd sent me home with a box of them. I ate *kataifi* for practically every meal for the next week, scooping them straight out of the box with a fork.

"I think that one is trying to get your attention," she said, after I'd made myself comfortable.

"Who?"

A him? In post post-menopausal city? Men in other countries might be progressive and secure enough in their masculinity to admit that knitting and crochet aren't women-exclusive crafts, but Greek men grab their balls and refuse to make eye contact with anything that might be yarn for fear they might start bleeding once a month and crying over something other than sports.

My gaze skimmed the room.

Oh boy, it was the little guy—Kontos. What was he doing in a knitting group? I craned my neck an inch further and saw that he was indeed knitting. Fat needles, green yarn.

And he said he wasn't a leprechaun.

I scratched my nose with my middle finger.

He flipped me off with both hands.

"Do you knit, my doll?" Kyria Kalliope's needles continued their metallic clicking.

"No. I'm a big fan of sweaters and scarves though," I said optimistically. "Does that count?"

My mother had tried to teach Toula and me to teach one winter. Toula took to it immediately and later went on to knit baby clothes for my niece and nephew. Me ... well ... let's just say I'd rather drive the needles through my own forehead than knit-and-purl.

She made a clucking sound. "Knitting is not just about sweaters. This piece is an afghan. It is for a competition."

My eyes slid to the red yarn moving backwards and forwards across the needles. "What competition is that?"

On the other side of the room, Kontos was scratching his forehead with his middle finger.

I scratched mine.

"Oh, it is a very important competition. We have it every Christmas. This year I am making the winner."

The Winter Fair. Of course. "Do you always enter?"

"Every year since I was a girl. But I never win. Maybe this year." Her face remained serene.

"Kyria Olga has won a few of them."

The needles slowed and she sighed. "For nearly fifty years, Olga has won first prize almost every winter. But this year will be different. Did you see her piece last year? Nothing special."

I knew the piece. It hung above the bed in Kyria Olga's spare bedroom. White wooly angels clung to a heavenly angora backdrop, watching over whomever occupied the bed below. I remembered now how proud she had been to place her blue ribbon in a leather album she kept for such mementos, all the time insisting that it was no big thing. Which member of the Maroulis clan would toss it in the trash first? There was no shame amongst vultures.

"Did Kyria Olga ever mention an argument she'd had with anyone recently?"

Her eyes lit up and the needles stopped clacking. A smile accompanied her words.

"Olga? Do you know her?" The smile faded slightly as she glanced around the room. "I wonder where she is today? She always comes on Saturday."

Dementia? Alzheimer's?

It would be hopeless and cruel to probe her further. Instead, I sat with her for a while discussing baked goods before moving on. I worked the room, one eye on Kontos, who seemed to have some permanent problem with his middle finger. Perhaps someone needed to snap it off for him.

Just as I thought I'd never get away from a pair of old women who decided I looked like I needed fifty different recipes for okra and chickpeas, my phone buzzed. I excused myself—flicking Kontos's ear as I pushed past—and answered the phone.

"Where is my mother's milk?"

Athena, in all her genteel glory. "How did you get this number?"

"I want the milk."

I rolled my eyes. Too bad she couldn't see it. "It's in my fridge."

"I will find a way to open your door."

There was a click then dead air. When her words registered, I freaked. There was no telling what Athena might resort to. She could be picking the lock right now. She could be eating the door.

I bolted.

CHAPTER SEVEN

Athena was doing a convincing imitation of a prison guard, barring my door with her considerable bulk. Even from a distance I could tell she meant business, and would probably injure me if I didn't hand over the milk.

I contemplated putting her in a headlock and shoving the container in a very dark place.

"If you're listening, Kyria Olga, please forgive me if I do something cruel and unnatural to your firstborn," I muttered.

Athena scowled. "I want my mother's milk."

The devil in me wasn't going to make this easy. "I paid for that milk you know, so technically it's mine."

"The Virgin Mary hates dirty liars."

I'd been called worse things by better people. "You can have it ..."

"Good."

"... if you pay for it."

"*Mounoskeelo!*"

So now I was a dog's private parts? Lovely.

"Let me think. It cost four euros and twenty-three cents.

Of course, you might want to give me the correct money because I can't make change."

She turned purple. Any more and she'd blow out an artery. How would I explain that to Kyria Olga ... and the police?

"Okay," I said, jingling my keys. "I'll get it for you."

She shifted to the right. Her breath brushed my neck. Oh no, was she going to follow me in?

I wagged a finger at her. "Wait there." I slipped through the cracked door and slammed it behind me, slapping the security chain into place just in case she decided to press the issue and hurl her weight against the wood.

All kinds of things ran through my head, the cleanest of which was spitting into the milk container. It wasn't usually my modus operandi to be vindictive, but she was bringing out the worst in me.

No. I wasn't going to be that person.

I removed the milk from the refrigerator, poured in a little tap water to replace the fraction Toula had used, and shook the bottle.

There. She would never know the difference.

When I was done I slipped out the front door again.

Nostrils flaring, Athena snatched the bottle from my hands. "Only the Virgin Mary knows what else you have stolen from my mama, but I will find out. I know your type."

She clomped back inside and slammed the door. Whether she was peeping though the spy hole or not, I didn't care. I raised the middle fingers on both hands and gave her the dual Greek wave.

"I saw that."

I jumped back and spun around. Kyria Olga's transparent head poked through my front door.

"Any chance you could announce your arrival? Maybe you could rattle some chains, or make those ghost noises. You know ... woo-woo." I wiggled my fingers.

Her head disappeared with a visual pop, and when I opened my apartment door she was inside, waiting.

"For your information, I cannot apply to get chains until I have been dead for at least a hundred years. Chain envy is prevalent in the afterlife, and stealing someone else's chains carries a very high price."

Who knew? "What if you just borrow them for a bit?"

Her lavender-tipped head shook as she pursed her lips disapprovingly. "The penalty is soul-death."

"Soul death?"

She drew a line across her neck. "The most permanent kind of death. They burn the souls in a magic incinerator."

A magic incinerator? Really? "Maybe just a polite cough?"

"How? I do not have lungs."

I snapped my hair back in a ponytail, getting ready to work. "Lack of lungs doesn't stop you from talking non-stop."

With a tap, my laptop woke from its nap. I clicked open a new spreadsheet and entered every tiny detail and suspicion that had zipped around inside my head so far. Which was basically nothing. But I did add the names of everyone I'd met at the knitting group, Kyria Olga's children, and the man who obviously had a crush on her.

Kyria Olga hovered behind me watching my fingers fly over the keyboard. She clapped. "I knew it. You are going to solve my murder."

"I'm doing this to preserve my sanity," I said, entering my list of possible motives. "The sooner your family leaves, the more peaceful my life will be. They're leeches."

There was a small pinging noise and she turned back into the sphere. The gold ball floated over to the desk where it hovered over a pile of folders. That was the good thing about being a ghost, I guess, you couldn't knock things over.

"They are vultures, all of them. And Athena's husband is a *mouni*," said the sphere.

"Olga Marouli! I didn't know you used words like that."

"I never used to, but it is true. And my granddaughter is a *putana*."

I stopped typing in the Maroulis' names and glanced over at her. "Lydia? She's not with the rest of them. Any idea where she is?"

"I am a ghost, not a god."

"Fine. I don't suppose she killed you? Because it would make my job easier if she did."

"Just write *putana* next to her name." She leaned forward and pointed at the screen. "They are all spending their lives swatting flies, waiting for me to die. Oh, I do love them, but they have made it very difficult for me to like any of them. Except Lydia. That girl has always had fire in her ... and more than a few firemen."

My chin dipped lower as I bit my lip and squelched a smile.

She zipped around my apartment then hovered beside me. "I am going to see if they are fighting over my things yet. My funeral is on Monday, and then the reading of my will afterwards. Then you will really see their true colors. I expect them to put on a good show, maybe even shed some fake tears. Maybe even ... blood!" She was practically quivering with excitement. The sphere shimmered and she was back again.

"I'll let Detective Samaras know there might be some problems."

She fanned her face. "He is a handsome devil."

My shoulders rose in a half-hearted shrug. "He's not bad. From what I hear—" pointed at the ceiling "—lots of other women think he's not too bad either."

"Yes, but it was your *kolos* he was staring at today when he was here."

I blocked my ears with two fingers. "La-la-la, I can't hear you."

"Since you are being so stubborn, I am going to see what activities are going on in the Afterlife. I am hoping to organize a Bingo club."

I unblocked my ears and paid attention to my trackpad, which was suddenly sluggish. Blowing hard, I let my breath push hair off the surface. Cat hair. Weird.

"What are you going to use for prizes? I'm guessing meat packs are out of the question, given that you've all given up meat." I wiggled my finger, and this time the cursor slid smoothly across the screen.

She batted her eyelashes and smiled. "I am looking at it."

Slowly, her words seeped in and I groaned. "No. Hell no."

"The deceased have problems too, you know."

"I have enough live clients without having to help out the dead ones! The living ones pay the rent!"

She clicked her fingers and disappeared in a small flash of golden light.

Show off.

———

The evening was far more fruitful. Almost simultaneously the phone rang and my email pinged.

Angela Zouboulaki, a regular client and one of Merope's more affluent women, called in a torrent of tears, begging me to find whether her relatively new amore was the real deal or a cheating jerk just waiting to stick his paws in her purse.

Decent money for easy work.

I said yes and jotted down some basic information while she emailed me a photograph of her lover. One Pavlos Mavros. Middle aged. Attractive in a slick, predatory way. But I had been fooled before, and sometimes I went back to a client with a report that their partner was faithful and that he--or she—was spending their spare time taking dancing classes or raising money for blind school children.

Expect everything. Now that's a motto to live by.

I clicked the phone off and turned back to the waiting email. The sender was a Jimmy K.

I found your card on the message board at the More Super Market. I'm looking for a woman with a clean body and a dirty mouth. Bonus points if she's a little person like me. I'm looking for permanent, not temporary—Jimmy Kontos

Holy seagull poop on a statue! Jimmy K. was the obnoxious little snot who'd kicked me. A suitable reply would take time—time I didn't have right now.

I grabbed my bag and trudged downstairs.

There are a five places where a person can do serious drinking in Merope. That is, five within the village itself and that aren't classified as *tavernas*, where you can get a fantastic meal to go with those drinks. Only two of those are places I would frequent if I was into drinking myself into oblivion in a smoke-filled, pervert-stacked environment. Work forced me through the doors of both places least once each month.

Bars aren't so great for picking up casual gossip; too much noise and too much drinking going on. The real action is outside, where you can get almost anything out of a person who is this side of inebriation. Some people might call that taking advantage of an unfortunate situation, but I just consider myself resourceful.

One of the remaining three bars is the type of place the fashionable residents of Merope go to see and be seen. There's music of the electronic blips, beeps and throbbing bass variety, and multilayered drinks with fancy names like, Douche Canoe, Lava Lamp, and my personal favorite, Jack The Ripper.

Number four and five on the list are outhouses. If you

don't get stabbed, molested, or robbed on the way to the
bathroom, be grateful and leave; there won't be any second
chances to escaped unscathed.

Feeling optimistic, I started at the top of the desirability
list. Why face a stabbing unless it's absolute absolutely
necessary?

I strolled casually across the road to The Good Time as if
I wanted nothing more than to be shown a good time by a
drunk man with retsina breath and a comb-over. The place
was packed with warm bodies. I squeezed through the crowd,
waved to a familiar face or two, and leaned an elbow against
the bar.

The bartender chucked his chin at me. "Hey, Callas,
what's it going to be?"

Paris the bartender is a wiry bald guy with homemade
tattoos stamped up and down the visible bits of his body. We
were in school together, from kindergarten to graduation.
Paris is appealing if you regularly entertain a prison-sex
fantasy. I don't, but other women love him—especially tourist
women. They skulk back to the bar after their husbands go to
bed, carefully ditching their wedding rings along the way.

"Coke. On the rocks."

He snorted in disgust, filled a highball from the soda gun
and slid it across the bar. "Catch."

I dropped a couple of euros on the bar. "Thanks."

Sipping slowly, I sized up the place. Nothing had changed
since I was in here on a similar evening a month earlier. Same
crowd, same smell, and the same boppy tunes.

There was no sign of Angela's wayward lover at the bar, so
I squeezed past the wall of people, drink in hand, and pushed
through to the back where several booths and tables provided
a safe space for those who wanted to yell at each other or play
I'll Touch Yours if You Touch Mine.

There was no sign of him there either. One bar down, four to go.

Someone bumped me from behind. I turned around and zeroed in on a table tucked around a nearly private corner. Two people sat close, heads together, mouths this close to kissing.

I didn't recognize the woman, but I knew the man: Detective Leo Samaras.

CHAPTER EIGHT

My feet froze and my gaze locked onto the couple. Bugs skittered around in my stomach. What was my problem? I'd met him two times in a strictly professional capacity—one while I wasn't fit for human consumption. So why did I feel like I'd just taken a punch in the boob? It wasn't like this was a surprise; I already knew he was a life support system for a penis. His bed springs sang the same song on a regular basis, day and night.

I didn't stick around to analyze my ridiculous reaction. I turned on one heel and bolted out to the street, where I realized my fingers were still clutching the half-full highball.

Performing Olympics-worthy mental gymnastics, I rationalized the whole non-encounter by telling myself that I would have been wasting my client's time if I'd hung around to say hello when her boyfriend clearly wasn't skulking around that particular bar.

Yeah, that was it.

Loser.

(Me, that is.)

I sprinted to the next bar. By the time I reached the front

door I believed my own bullshit. Also: new highball glass. That was a good thing, right?

Merope's Misfortune is a decorating monstrosity. It's filled with every stereotypical Greek thing ever. The Parthenon's facade out front. Pillars in clashing styles. Too much blue and white. The staff dress like Greek fishermen and wear stick-on mustaches. Even the women.

Eager to get the evening over, I skipped the idle small talk with the mustachioed bartender and did a quick circuit of the bar. It was crowded, which obscured most of the puke-worthy décor.

I hit pay dirt at the back of the crowded quarters.

Angela's love-monkey was hunkered down at a table with four other men. The waitress must have been run off her feet elsewhere because the table was crowded with empties, about five apiece. Just an innocent boys night out without so much as a g-stringed butt in sight.

Nursing my coke, I worked my way back to the bar and waited until a bar stool emptied. I pounced before it could cool down. From this vantage point I could keep both eyes on Pavlos Mavros with minimal effort, and he couldn't leave without skulking past me. While I shot furtive glances at Angela's boyfriend I played Candy Crush and lamented my single status. I'm not a hopeless case when it comes to men. Most of my relationships have been longterm, and Andreas and I were this close to the altar before it ended abruptly in crushing heartache. But the past couple of years had been a wasteland; slim pickings and runts of the litter.

The older I got, the harder it was getting to find a decent single man. And just because a man said he was single, didn't mean it was the truth.

Olga was right, Detective Samaras was definitely a catch, and some part of me was definitely interested. But it was a moot point now anyway. He was a fisherman and I didn't want to be one of his fish. I'd had my fill of bad boys. If I was desperate for anything, it was a healthy helping of nice.

Someone shoved a coin in the jukebox and a band from 90s began to play. I sat and crossed my fingers that lover-man would get up soon and leave. I was desperate to crawl into bed and put the day behind me. Wrapped in fresh sheets and warm covers, the whole world would seem better.

Finger-crossing worked.

Across the room, Pavlos Mavros stood. He worked his way past me in a retsina-fueled ballet of weaving and stumbling.

This time I left the highball behind.

He was clearly plastered, tripping, swaying and fumbling with his keys. He probably had a nasty case of brewer's droop to go along with the inebriation. No skirt chasing for lover-man tonight, which would make my client happy.

I punched her digits on my cell phone. She answered on the second ring.

"Do you want the good news or the bad?"

"He's cheating, isn't he? I just know it. Is it that *mouni* who works at the bakery?"

For the record, the so-called *mouni* at the bakery was an out-and-proud lesbian, so I was fairly sure that Pavlos wasn't banging her.

"Guess again."

Angela sighed dramatically. "Give me the good, then soften the bad. Pound it with a hammer first if you have to."

Right. "Your new guy seems to be faithful, at least tonight. He really was out with the boys."

"Was?" She sounded puzzled.

"Well, the bad news is that right now I'm watching him stumble to his car. I doubt if he'll be able to get the key in. You want me to call him a cab?"

"That *malakas*," she said, sounding relieved. "Give the cab driver some money and I'll reimburse you."

The next number I dialed was the cab company. It was Pavlos's lucky night—the cab was close by. Its lights lit the parking lot up almost immediately.

I trotted over to where he was fumbling with the keys. He dropped them. I bent down to pick them up and pocketed them.

"Pavlos? Angela asked me to get you a cab. Come on."

A lot of men might have been resistant, but Pavlos was pliant. He seemed slightly bewildered as he followed me to the cab.

"Who are you?" he slurred.

"I'm you guardian angel."

"Where are your wings?"

"They're invisible."

"Good idea."

"Sometimes I have them," I said.

He climbed into the backseat of the cab without any protest. I shoved his keys in the pocket of his leather jacket. I gave the driver Angela's address and slipped him a ten.

Maybe I'd saved a life or two tonight, and possibly a relationship.

———

Knocking woke me up. That's a common occurrence when one lives in an apartment building. But this morning it was my door being hammered upon by a rain of fists. Or, as I discovered when I peeped through the spy hole, two overly enthusiastic fists.

Athena.

Why me?

"Come back later," I shouted through the door. "I'm busy."

"Have you got a man in there?" The thick door muffled her voice.

What kind of question was that? And what business was it of hers anyway?

"Yes," I lied. "And he's doing unspeakable things to me right now. It's all very appalling. I should probably go to church, but not until he's done doing this thing he's doing."

"I want to borrow some bread," she said, raising her voice.

"I only eat bread, I don't loan it out."

A cold whisper brushed my feet. I jumped backwards, stumbling, until the wall caught my back. A cat had appeared out of nowhere, waving the tip of his fuzzy orange tail. He blinked his big green eyes as if to ask, *What's the fuss all about?*

Now I remembered him. He'd come calling the other night when I was drowning in ouzo.

"I've seen you before, haven't I?" I kept my voice low. "Where did you come from?"

His tail thumped faster. After spinning around to face the door, he let out a low growl. "If you're really my friend, you'll go out there and pee on the bad woman's leg."

"I heard that!" Athena bellowed.

The tail stiffened. Things weren't looking good for Athena.

"Go get her," I whispered

Dead Cat leaped through the door.

Eye against the peephole, I watched. He circled her twice. Sniffed. Backed up, squatted slightly, and let a stream of bright yellow pee hit her shoe.

Athena stumbled backwards. "*Gamo tin putana sou!* What did you do to me? I know it was you!"

It's not easy to feel guilty and laugh at the same time, but

I managed to multitask, leaning against the door with a fist jammed against my teeth so the laugh wouldn't leak out.

Something heavy banged against the door. I peeped out again. Athena kicked the door a second time and turned on her heel. A moment later the door to 201 slammed shut.

I opened my door and sniffed. Athena might have felt the pee but I sure couldn't smell it. And there was no patch of liquid on the marble; it was gone along with the cat.

My life was getting weirder by the minute.

The idea of crawling back into bed crossed my mind, but it was hopeless. The sun was up and poking its fingers through the shutters. I pulled on clean jeans, coupling them with a thin black sweater and dashed across the street to Merope's Best for some of Merope's worst. The coffee shop's beans were always burnt, giving their coffee the taste of oven scrapings—or at least what I imagined oven scrapings might taste like if I ever got a sudden craving to lick the inside of a scorched roasting tray. Yet many locals flocked there for fancy coffees, rather than hit the *kafeneios* for the regular Greek menu.

"I can't believe you keep coming back for this *skata*," the teenage barista said.

"Self-flagellation. I just did something very wrong."

"Yeah, me too."

I hoped it didn't involve my coffee.

When the coffee slid across the counter, I poured a mountain of sugar into the liquid and stirred. After a sip I decided it was almost drinkable. Coffee in one hand, newspaper tucked under my arm, I trotted back across the street.

"My beautiful new neighbor," someone said. I tried not to flinch; George Maroulis was headed my way, minus his offspring and siblings. A shit-eating grin spread across his bland features.

I was trapped.

"Good morning, George. I didn't realize we were neighbors now."

I knew what he meant, but I was feeling antagonistic after his sister's hammering woke me up.

George's smile dimmed slightly then regained its full brightness. He pointed at me. "You. You are a funny one."

"It's all part of the wonderfulness of me. I'm thinking about doing some standup comedy." He stared back blankly so I added, "How are you and your boys coping?"

It could have been the sunlight causing irritation to his pale eyeballs or it could have been grief that caused his eyes to redden and well with tears. Two palms up, he shrugged. "The boys are good. They are boys, you know? They were never close to Mama."

"And you? How are you coping?" I asked quietly, feeling a jab of pity for my friend's son.

"I will be fine." He gave a half wave and turned toward the coffee shop. He shook his head slightly as if his ears were filled with water. "Thank you for being there for my mother."

Just when you think you've got someone pegged. "She was a good woman."

He gave me a damp smile, and we went our separate ways. At least there was one Marouli sibling who possessed a sliver of humanity.

Despite my line of work, I'm not an overly paranoid person. I don't believe big brother is always watching and I don't believe someone is out to get me. You won't find a tin foil hat hanging in my closet. Nevertheless, for the sake of self preservation, I crept up the stairs and peeked down the hall to make sure no other members of the Marouli family were lurking in the corridors waiting to hold me hostage.

All clear.

I crept all the way to my front door, taking particular care not to rattle the keys.

Yes! I was home free.

I did a little victory dance, the move Toula calls my 'hoochie dance' on account of how it involves what kids these days call twerking. I rump-jiggled into the kitchen, pulled the last orange cupcake out of the Cake Emporium box and flipped the newspaper's pages. My fingertips turned black from the print after just a couple of turns. In a few minutes I'd covered the complete geography of Merope's paper. The letters to the editor were the only bright spots; here a citizen of the island could air their grievances without revealing their identity.

Today's letters shook their paper fists at rising gasoline prices (Greece's gasoline prices never went anyplace but up, thanks to outrageous taxes) and the incompetence of the police in solving the murder of Olga Marouli. Everybody on the island watched the same police procedurals as Athena, and now they were armchair experts.

Bored with the daily news, I shut my eyes and allowed myself to be carried away while my tongue prodded around my mouth, searching out stray blobs of cupcake.

Thump. Thump. Thump.

Thump after hip-thrusting thump.

The noise was coming from upstairs. Detective Leo Samaras's apartment.

The familiar squeaking began.

I rolled off the couch, tossed the newspaper on the coffee table. The last thing I wanted to do was sit and listen to his sex fest. I used to cheer him on, but that was before I developed a low-level crush.

The squeaking continued. I turned on the radio and cranked the music up, then turned it back down because the noise bugged me. I opened my laptop and tried to concentrate on Olga's slow-growing file.

It was no good. The squeaking was drilling into my head.

Enough was enough. I raced upstairs. Sexual healing or not, I didn't want to listen to his erotic escapades.

I braced myself for gratuitous nudity and knocked on the door of 302. It was identical to my own, but the air up here felt different. I pressed an ear to the door and listened. Talking? A television. And the squeaking. It was fainter out here. He probably had no idea how loud it was in my apartment below.

I knocked again.

The squeaking stopped. Footsteps slapped the floor, and the door opened. I braced myself for anything—possibly nothing, and by nothing I meant nudity.

A sweaty Leo Samaras filled the doorway. No shirt. Loose cotton shorts. Glistening caramel body. My eyes dropped down to his sneakers clad and back up to his bare chest. It was as broad and muscular as I imagined. I gulped and fought the hot flash.

Slow on the uptake, I began to put two and two together.

No sweaty, vigorous sex.

Vigorous workout, yes. But not sex.

My mouth opened and closed as my brain ticked over.

"Everything okay, Allie?" His brow crumpled. His hazel eyes clouded over.

"Never mind." I pivoted on one foot.

"Wait. Is this about Olga Marouli?"

It was my turn to frown. "No. Actually I was just coming up to make a monumental dick of myself. I'm just going to go now before I embarrass both of us."

When I met his eyes, he was grinning.

"What?"

"Nothing," he said. "It's early. You want to come in for coffee?"

"Thanks, but I have a cup of Merope's Worst waiting for me downstairs." I trotted downstairs with pep in my step. By the time I reached my own door my mood had lifted. Seeing Leo Samaras alone had accomplished what Merope's Worst couldn't.

It didn't last. Just my luck.

A door that wasn't mine clicked.

"You. I want to talk to you."

My face burned. This was a deadly Athena booby-trap. Slowly, I turned around to face her. "What can I do for you this time, Athena?"

Her face was flushed and not at all flattered by the blue polyester with pink nylon flamingoes. Still no black. Her mother's favorite baubles dangled in her fleshy lobes. The same ones that always adorned her ears for church on Sundays.

"Nice earrings," I said dryly. My contempt bubbled just below the surface.

Her eyes narrowed as if I'd insulted her but she couldn't quite figure out how. "You are a private investigator."

Where was she going with this? "Not even close."

"That is what they told me."

"*They* are mistaken."

"You should be trying to find my mother's killer," she said. Her eyes dared me to protest.

"You're mistaking me for the police. Their number is in the phone book. Detective Samaras gave you his card. Call." I pushed my door open.

"Mama was your friend. You have an obligation."

"Are you saying you want to hire my services?"

"Hire? You mean pay you money?"

Somebody forgot to stand in line when they were giving people a clue.

"I generally ask for a retainer."

"A retainer." Her face blanked as she processed my words.

"Yes. It's a sum of money paid to retain my services."

"How much?"

I gave her my very modest rate, with an extra ten percent tacked on for Pain in the Ass tax.

Her eyes bulged. "That is theft!"

"That's the price of doing business."

A roar erupted through the door of 201. Athena's chest heaved.

"These apartments are not very big," she went on. "It is cramped with the six of us. We will need to borrow your shower."

There seemed to be no limit to Athena's lack of social niceties.

"No," I said, pressing as hard as I could on the word.

Her mouth kept moving. It didn't seem to be connected to her brain.

"And because it is just you living there, one of the children could sleep on your couch. You do not need all this room to yourself. Mama would have wanted you to help her children in our time of need."

My right eye twitched. "Still no."

"We have decided you are going to host the wake tomorrow. We do not have the space, and because we have not got Mama's money yet, we are a little tight financially. I will give you instructions later."

She had to be kidding me.

Her fleshy jaw was set. Her eyes bored into mine.

My parents didn't raise me to be a liar. That was a skill I picked up later in the third grade when I pulled down a classmate's pants to see what he was hiding down there. Turned out not much. Still, I concocted an elaborate lie involving tripping on a tree root and grasping onto the closest anchor. The principal gave me a week of detention anyway, and the boy in question went on to have five children, so obviously I hadn't damaged him for life.

Fortunately, Athena was a whole lot dumber than my elementary school principal. I could give my lie a little twist of flair.

"I don't think so. I have anthrax And ebola. You probably wouldn't want to use my bathroom because that whole bleeding out the ears, and eyes, and nose can get pretty gross. Plus the oozing ... it's icky and definitely infectious." I leapt back into my apartment and slammed the door.

I stormed into the living room, hands on hips, teeth grinding together.

"Olga Marouli, you get down here right now," I hissed. Silence stagnated in the air. I tried another tactic, it was time to play dirty. "After they bury you, I'll visit your grave every day and sing. And," I said, sticking the knife in deep and twisting, "I'll tell Athena that Stavros Psaris was in love with you."

CHAPTER NINE

Poof!

Olga appeared, washed in a golden glow.

"Aliki Callas, I never knew you could be so cruel," she said, giving me a haughty look.

See? I only hear my first name when I'm in trouble.

"Live and learn."

"That is a terrible thing to say to a dead person," she said sourly.

I waved my hands, Greek-style. "Call it an act of desperation and bone-crushing anxiety. And given that the source of my anxiety is your daughter, I feel like it's necessary to involve you. Can't you send her to her room or something?"

"You interrupted an exciting game of bingo. I was about to call out eighty-eight, two-fat-ladies."

My eyes narrowed. "Are you still gambling with my time?"

She sighed. "No. I cannot believe how backwards the Afterlife is sometimes. Can you believe gambling for goods is against the rules? A group of us are petitioning, but we have only got three million signatures so far. We need at least 2 billion to get a shot at being heard."

I shook my head. I didn't dare ask what would happen next. Maybe it was one of those non-negotiable things. Like taxes. "Well that's certainly proactive."

"Those lovely Rat Pack men are among our biggest campaigners. They want to build a casino."

"The Rat Pack," I said faintly.

"Dino, Sammy, and Frankie too." She sighed dreamily and shook her head. A faraway look clouded her eyes. "That Frankie, they say he is hung like an elephant. One of the bigger elephants from Africa."

My eye twitched. It was doing that a lot lately. "About Athena ..."

Kyria Olga eyes snapped back to me. "What has she done now?"

I filled her in on Athena's demands. As I ran down the list her eyes grew wider and her mouth dropped into a loose O.

"I raised a monster," she said breathlessly. "She is a monster. A stupid monster. She could drown in a teaspoon of water. Tell her to *klasimo* on your *archidia*."

"I can't say that!"

I mean, I wanted to tell Athena no and that she couldn't do anything about it, but I wasn't going to do it the Greek way, telling her she could fart on my balls.

"Why not? I would."

"There must be something I can do or say to stop her in her tracks." I shot her my most pleading and desperate look. Desperate people do desperate things.

"Athena is my eldest child but my eyes are wide open when it comes to seeing both the good and the bad inside of her. I had high hopes for her: a good college, a career, and a strong man. Instead what did she do? She marries that *malakas* who dribbled down the back of his *baba's* leg."

I would never look at Athena's beige husband the same way again. "I guess she made her choices," I said.

"Would you do me a favor?"

"Nearly anything. I do have some limits."

She gave me a funny look. "Say no to the wake, and make sure they do not embarrass me at my funeral. I could not handle it if they made a spectacle. No big wailing speeches about how I was their dear mama and how much they loved me. It is a load of *skata*."

"I'm sure they won't," I said, lying through my teeth. Athena struck me as someone who excreted drama through her pores.

"They will find a way."

The doorbell chimed. We both glanced at the door.

"That better not be your daughter again. This time she'll probably want me to move out and leave my apartment completely furnished at her disposal." Only half of me was joking.

Olga floated over to the door and pushed her head through the panels, all the way up to the shoulders. A twinge of queasiness shot through me.

She pulled it back and shot me a satisfied grin. "It is the nice policeman from upstairs."

My gut clenched. Butterflies committed *seppuku* in my stomach. "Is he dressed?"

"Yes, and that is the real crime here."

"Are you going to stay and make polite conversation with us?"

"Conversation? No."

The doorbell chimed again. This time I opened up.

Kyria Olga was telling the truth: it was Detective Samaras —Leo—and he was dressed in faded jeans and an equally faded t-shirt. He did things for old clothes that ought to be illegal.

"Am I interrupting?" he asked, peering past me.

"No."

"I heard voices."

"Television. It rots the brain, but it's good company while I work."

Way to go, genius. Stun him with your scintillating witticisms. Next I'd probably find myself reciting my shopping list or the literature in a tampon box.

"I like TV," he said. "Maybe that's what's wrong with my brain. What was that all about at my apartment?"

"Nothing, I told you."

He crossed his arms, moved his legs into the at-ease position. He was shooting for casual but wound up looking more intimidating than usual. "Make it easy on yourself and tell the truth. I'm a whiz in the interrogation room."

I bet you are, I thought. "Blackmail? Isn't that illegal?"

"Only if you file a complaint." His lips curved into a sexy smile, and despite wanting to remain cool, I returned it.

"It was silly."

"We could play your favorite game, twenty questions."

My face burned. "Fine, you win. I was trying to work, and there was a lot of ... thumping and squeaking going on, so I couldn't concentrate."

"I was working out. My treadmill is in the ..." he trailed off and made a face. "I'm an inconsiderate *malakas*, aren't I?"

"No ..."

"Say it. You know you want to."

"It's nothing," I said.

"It's something."

"I didn't realize it was your treadmill."

He said nothing.

"I thought you were ... you know."

"No, I don't know. Not a mindreader."

"To use an English word: *bonking*."

"I know what *bonking* means."

"And then I saw you last night with that woman at the The Good Time ..."

He lowered his chin and swallowed a smile. "So why did you come upstairs if you thought I was ... busy?"

"I was just coming to check on your welfare. Wouldn't want you to be too exhausted to work."

This time he laughed. "Fair enough." He flipped a thumb at the door behind him. "They still there? Never mind, the look on your face says it all."

"Am I that transparent?"

"No, they're that awful," he said in a stage-whisper. "Athena was down at the station last night, giving Pappas hell. He was crying by the time she left."

Poor Pappas. He was just a kid, and I already felt sorry for him after the vomiting incident.

The front door to 201 flew open and Athena appeared, nostrils flaring. Was she camping out in a chair by the door, ready to pounce on unsuspecting tenants?

This time she wasn't alone.

Vera, in her chemical haze, followed behind at a speed that was best described as fifty percent off regular speed. If possible she appeared to be thinner and more pale that she had yesterday. Probably Athena was sucking the life out of her siblings.

Leo paled until his skin was as washed-out as his clothes. I had to hand it to him though, his expression remained consistent. I wished I could stay that cool. Maybe if I asked nicely he'd give me stoicism lessons.

"Detective," Athena whined.

Leon nodded curtly. "What can I do for you today?"

The full-figured woman squared her shoulders and prepared for attack. Poor Leo. Homicidal axe murderers were pansies compared to Athena.

A soft snort worked its way out of my nose. Athena's gaze cut to me. Her eyes narrowed.

I covered it up with a cough. "Allergies," I said.

"Detective, have you caught my mama's murderer yet?"

"We're working on it, day and night."

"It does not look me like you are working on anything except putting your *poutsa* in garbage. Why aren't you out working? The murderer could come back at any moment and kill us all where we sleep."

Leo's color came back. "Since I've got you here, I can save you another trip to the station and ask you a few questions." There was a soft scratching as he ran a hand over his five-o'clock shadow. "Come to think of it, we need you to come downtown anyway, to give DNA samples."

Vera's eyes flickered into focus then drifted back into fog. Athena's mouth collapsed into a grim hard line. I took a step back, just in case.

"You cannot possibly think one of us is responsible," Athena said in disbelief.

"If there's one thing I've learned, it's that family members have the most to profit from death. Your family is probably no different." His mouth twitched ever so slightly.

"That is a terrible thing to say!" she hissed. Her eyes bugged and I had the distinct feeling tears or bodily injury to those of us around her weren't too far away.

"It goes with the investigation, along with full background checks on all family members."

She recoiled. "You would not do that!"

"We already did. That's where I'm going now. Apparently there's something interesting I need to see."

Athena froze.

"If I were you," he continued. "I would go to church and pray, and then meet me at the police station. It's your lucky day. Services start," he glanced at his watch, "in half an hour."

Church. Olga Marouli was a weekly worshiper at Ayios Konstantinos—Saint Constantine. Every Sunday, she donned a black dress and pearls and strolled down the block to the 10:00 A.M service.

Detective Samaras and Athena were in a standoff, and as far as I could see, only one of them had a gun. I placed my bet on Leo. What can I say; I'm an optimist. Any second now, one of those crazy kids was going to stand down and leave me free to run back into my own apartment and change clothes. I held onto the thought that Olga's killer was someone in her social circle. Maybe the circumstances of her death were hazy but it didn't take much to see that either she opened the door for someone she knew, or that perhaps someone was close enough to her that they had their own key.

Which reminded me ...

"Athena, how did you get the key to your mother's apartment?"

Her death-rays were still focused on the detective. "Nobody gave me the key. You and this one were inside and the door was unlocked."

"You don't have your own key?"

Her eyes slid over to meet mine. "No." They immediately flicked back to Leo.

"Vera, how about you?"

"Mama never gave out keys," she said in a dazed voice. How much of that stuff was she popping anyway? I wondered what her blood to diazepam ratio was.

I wasn't entirely convinced. As soon as Olga Marouli reappeared, I'd ask her about keys. In the meantime I was going to do something nice.

"Detective Samaras," I said in my sweetest sugar-dipped voice. "I have that information you asked for. Come on in and I'll walk you through it."

Anyone else might have registered sweet relief, but the cool detective's face remained neutral. "Thank you Despinida Callas. The department appreciates it," he ad-libbed.

Athena wasn't done torturing us. "I want Mama's jewelry back. She always wore our family heirlooms."

Detective Samaras nodded curtly and turned back toward me.

"Her jewelry?" I asked.

"Athena made it very clear last night that she wants the jewelry her mother was wearing when she was killed."

I shot Athena in the face with the evil eye. That woman was just too much. I pushed the door open and stepped inside.

Leo followed.

Just before I shut the door, I shoved the knife in and wiggled it around.

"Oh, Athena, I'd invite you in but I hear you're needed down at the police station."

Athena turned purple. Her chest heaved. Meanwhile, Tina was oblivious, staring into thin air at something only she could see.

Strange family.

"You can wait here until it's safe," I said, after I shut the door. I waved toward a chair and darted into the bedroom where I found black pants to go with my sweater. I squeezed my feet into pointy pumps with a modest heel and ran a brush through my hair. It would do for church, with the added bonus that I could run in these low heels if my well-being suddenly depended on it.

Plus they doubled as potentially lethal weapons. Practical and attractive.

Back in the living room, Leo was making himself comfortable--too comfortable--in front of my computer.

I cleared my throat.

Instead of looking guilty, his face broke into one of those slow grins that I swear men do on purpose. He nodded toward the open document on my screen.

"I thought you were going to leave this investigation to me?"

I reached past him and closed the lid. "I'm not close to a lot of people, I've told you that. Kyria Olga means a lot to me. I want ... need to do what ever I can to help her."

"You mean she *meant* a lot to you?"

"Means—present tense. I didn't give up caring just because she died."

"I'm sorry. Sometimes I just have to switch it off to get the job done."

"She asked me to help her if anything bad ever happened to her," I lied. "Simple as that. I'm just fulfilling her request. I'm discreet and I can promise that I won't do anything to compromise your investigation."

Leo rose from the swivel chair and put his hand on my shoulder. No doubt it was intended to comfort me, but instead it sent a series of pornographic images dancing through my mind. Seeking self-preservation—and dry under-wear—I stepped back.

"I promise if I dig up anything important, I'll pass it along. I'm used to dealing with the Merope police, just ask around."

"I already did." He shrugged. "Fine. Okay. Just leave the unnecessary risks to me. Anywhere else and I'd have to tell you to keep your nose out, but Merope is a small place and we're under-funded. Off the record, I could use all the help I can get."

I picked up my purse off the hallway table and slung it over one shoulder. "In that case, I have a date with the Father, the Son and Holy Spirit. It's possible I'll be stricken down before I even step foot in the door, so if I don't come back, look for the melted puddle of sludge just inside the church doors."

He laughed. "Not much of a churchgoer?"

"Only when I need a punch in the self-esteem."

CHAPTER TEN

We took the stairs. Leo stayed one step below me.

"Just in case you trip," he said.

The gesture wasn't lost on me. I rarely protest at chivalry.

"Are you trying to get on my good side?

"From what I can tell, all your sides are good." A buzz echoed in the stairwell. He grabbed the phone on his waistband and stopped. "Samaras."

I tried to hobble down past him but he put up an arm and mouthed, "Wait".

That's okay; I was only in a hurry.

"Who? Uh huh. I'll be right there."

His eyes narrowed as he focused on me. What did I do? Here I was, busy minding my own business and picking at a hangnail.

Leo clicked the phone off and shoved it back on to the waistband of his jeans. "I'll bet you know something about this."

"About what?"

"Dimitri Vlahos and Maria—"

"Stamatou," I finished. "And what makes you think I know anything about ... what exactly?"

He took my elbow and steered me to the bottom of the stairs. "Come with me."

"Why should I?"

"Just do it, trust me."

Intriguing.

I hopped into his black compact like a good little sheep. He stayed below the limit all the way to the moped rental place Vlahos owned, mostly because the traffic ahead of us was a weatherbeaten man on a browbeaten donkey.

My stomach started to churn. Nothing good was about to happen.

"What are you doing?"

Greeks ask what you're doing instead of how you are. Actions are gossip-worthy; feelings aren't.

"Waiting," I told him.

"Well, we're here."

Leo pulled up outside the rental place. Two patrol cars and an ambulance were parked just inside the gates. I couldn't see much more than that.

I glanced around, searching for some kind of clue. The street was empty except for Vasili Moustakas, who was wandering past with his wiener still hanging out. "Look at this!" he called out, and wrapped his scrotum around his penis until he'd made a hamburger. I laughed into my hand, magically transforming it into a cough at the last second.

I was back in control a moment later when Leo joined me.

"Don't touch anything, and I don't think I have to tell you to be discreet," he said in policeman mode.

"Yes, Detective."

He gave a quick smile before stashing it behind the cop veneer.

I trotted behind him, to where two cops including Gus Pappas were leaning on the trunk of a convertible. The paramedics were standing back, grinning. I glanced around quickly. Panos Grekos wasn't around, so there wasn't a dead body in that car.

Pappas was bright-eyed, almost levitating with excitement. "I have never seen anything like this. Too bad I can't Instagram it."

"No Instagram," Leo barked.

Pappas stepped aside so we could move around him.

"*Gamo tin Panayia mou*," Leo said, recommending that the Virgin Mary get laid as soon as possible.

I leaned forward and peered into the back seat of the convertible. Dimitri Vlahos was in a fix of the sexual kind, spread out on his back, shirt unbuttoned, pants and briefs shoved down around his ankles. My eyes closed in on the generous skid mark on his underwear. Looks like someone didn't get the hang of wiping.

But it was the rest of the picture that made me glad I wasn't drinking anything. Maria Stamatou was face down in pubic hair, and for some reason she wasn't getting up, although her arms were flailing around like quarter of a drunk octopus.

"*Vre gamisou*, what are you staring at?" Dimitri growled.

"I'm not really sure," I said and glanced at Leo. His face was unreadable. How did he do that?

"Are you *malakes* going to get me out of here or are you just going to stand around laughing?"

"We have to wait for the solvent," one of the paramedics said.

"Why can't you just lift them out onto a gurney?" I asked, without looking away from the train wreck.

"We tried, but they're stuck to the seat. Whatever we're going to do, we have to do it right here."

I leaned in closer. Was that blood?

"Strawberry lubricant," Pappas said, reading my mind. "Looks like Kyria Vlaho dosed it with superglue."

"Look on the bright side, Maria, maybe you can get a new pair of lips to match your new nose," I offered helpfully.

She flipped a red-tipped finger at me.

"The good news is that your new nose works," I added. "Yay, modern medicine."

Her lips made a weird sucking movement. I wouldn't testify to it in court, but I was pretty sure she was telling me to make sweet love to a farm animal.

Dimitri slapped at her head. "Quit that, *skeela*. You'e ripping my skin off!"

Maria's fist jumped up and crashed down on his face. Blood spurted in a thin arc, painting a scarlet ribbon on the upholstery. Dimitri's howl of bursting pain quickly turned into tears.

Gus Pappas roared with laughter. "*Malaka*, you were asking for that."

"I want to press charges," said Dimitri between sobs. Red snot bubbled out of his nose. I pulled a tissue out of my purse and dropped it on his face. He pressed it to his nose.

"This is all your fault, you *skeela*."

"Me? How's this my fault?" Was he high? This was so not my fault. "You're the one with a teenager stuck to your groin."

"My wife showed me the photos you took."

Oh, that.

Leo raised his brows and gave me a *told you so* look.

"She showed you the photos, yet you're still the one with your wobbly bits in someone who isn't your wife. You're the one making your own life a roller skate."

(Which is a Greek way of saying he was making his own life a living hell.)

"My wife is leaving me. She wants the business and she wants to keep me on as an employee. Me—an employee!

"Is she offering a good salary?" Pappas asked.

"Terrible."

A door slammed behind us. Panos Grekos the coroner lifted a large bucket of what looked like solvent out of his van.

"Do I look like a messenger boy to you?" he said to no one in particular.

It was probably time for me to leave since Dimitri was pissed and I was at the top of his shit list. Why make myself an easy target when I could get out of here now?

"I'd better go," I said to Leo.

He nodded. "Sure. You might want to keep a low profile for a while. If Dimitri bothers you, call me."

"I have pepper spray."

"And he has a grudge, which makes him more dangerous."

Leo took my hand. I thought it was a romantic gesture until it turned into a handshake at the last moment. "I'll check in on you later."

Grekos was hovering. "Samaras, you got a minute?"

Leo turned to pay attention the coroner.

I took my time, first pulling out my purse and pretending to check my cell messages. Snippets of the conversation reached my ears but I didn't perk up until the coroner said something about hair.

"A blonde hair?" Leo asked.

"Yeah, I bagged it and sent it to the lab."

"Good work. Is her body ready to be released?"

"Already gone."

So, they'd found a blonde hair. That was interesting.

I scurried away before the men realized I'd been eavesdropping ... but not before throwing an admiring gaze at Leo's buns of granite.

Ayios Konstantinos is quintessentially Greek. It's the subject of many a postcard, with its clean, white stucco and its bright blue dome. Inside it looks like King Midas went full Exorcist and projectile vomited gold, his head spinning like a top. At the front, Jesus Christ's eye-rolling expression said he couldn't believe he'd died for our sins because we were an ungrateful, wretched mob. I couldn't disagree with him.

The priest at Ayios Konstantinos is Father Spiros. He's older than dirt and colder than a penguin holding a popsicle, although he wears a sunny mask over the permafrost. Like many Greek priests he's not married, but he has a sister who performs an alarming number of wifely duties. And Kyria Sofia, the aforementioned sister, performs them with a minimum amount of human decency.

Thanks to Dimitri and Maria's amorous adventures with glue, I was running late and the service had already started. This meant that I would have to sneak in and hunker down in the back, behind as many bodies as possible.

Gathering my thoughts for a moment before sneaking inside, I closed my eyes. What exactly did I hope to learn here? Well, thanks to my eavesdropping skills I knew to start culling the blondes from the non-blondes. Other than that I would have to wing it.

"Kyria Olga?" I pulled out my phone so any stray onlookers wouldn't think I was holding a conversation with a non-ghost. "Any chance you can help me out here?"

Poof! Kyria Olga popped onto the church's steps. "What now?" She looked around. "Where is that delicious police-man? You two should be ..." She made an O with her finger and thumb and showed me exactly what she thought I should be doing with Leo.

"He had to go to work—on *your* case. How was bingo?"

She sighed. "It's just not the same. The thrill has gone. Even if you win ... so what?"

She had the afterlife blues, no doubt about it. "Maybe you're depressed."

"Post Death Blues. The handbook mentions it."

"Is there a treatment?"

"Just Ghostzac."

I blinked. "Really?"

"No. P.D.B. usually subside after you're buried, or in the case of a wrongful death, after the culprit is caught."

Now my motivation was twofold. "I'm working on it. In fact, you owe me one because I'm going to church for you."

"You talk like I am forcing you to go."

"You told me to investigate."

"Okay, okay. What can I do? Do you want me to shake things up a bit?" She shook her tail feathers. "Give them a show they will not forget? It is too bad I cannot make things move yet. I would love to see the look on Father Spiros's face if I grabbed his thurible and swung it around my head."

Wouldn't that be something?

"I need to know who you socialized with in church. I can't exactly waltz in there and just start questioning the whole congregation."

Her eyes twinkled dangerously. "You should do that. I would pay to see the looks on their faces when you ask if strangled me. The very thought of it would send their collective skirts flying up over their heads. Sofia would *kaka* her *sovraka* if someone suspected one of her brother's flock of being something as low-class as a murderer."

I know quite a lot about Kyria Sofia, and none of it is good if you grab a shovel and loosen the soil. Most weeks she's in the newspaper, usually posing next to Someone Very Important, wearing Something Modest, and talking about how she cares So Very Much about whatever it is she's supposed to be caring about at that moment.

The private Kyria Sofia is her evil twin. Bitching. Backstabbing. Betrayal. And that's just how she treats her friends and family.

And although I will never reveal my source, I can say that Kyria Sofia owns one of the largest bestiality porn collections in the country. She keeps it all hidden in computer folder labeled Sewing.

"Anyone else I should watch out for?"

"Keep your eye on all of them. They are snakes—and those are the good ones. And do not lose track of your purse. Father Spiros will have his fingers in it so fast you will not have time to kick him in the shins."

Something else popped into my head before I went in. "Did anyone else have a key to your apartment?"

"No. Why?"

I shook my head. "Never mind. It was a long shot anyway. Any chance you want to keep me company?"

Church isn't something I often do. When I show up it's for the usual reasons: Easter, baptisms, my mother's threats. I believe in God but I'm not sure He believes in me. On those rare occasions when I show up to church, it's never Ayios Konstantinos. I prefer the smaller Ayia Helena. It has less gold and more heart.

"I would not miss this for anything," Kyria Olga said cheerfully. She bobbed ahead of me, channeling a mylar balloon.

Father Spiros was up front, Bible open in his hands, his mouth moving at an exhausting speed. Nobody noticed me skulking in, and God must have been taking the day off again, because no holy death rays shot out of the sky to strike me dead. I was still living and breathing as I hid at the back near the icon of the Virgin Mary. Kyria Olga hovered next to me.

I eyed the rest of the worshipers. Slumping like this, all I could see were the backs of their coiffed heads. Across the aisle on the men's side, two boys were sitting on the floor, a Spiderman comic spread on the marble floor between them.

Maria Stamatou's parents were near the front. They'd be horrified when they found out where their daughter was right now, but not as horrified they would be when they realized their money couldn't squash this story. A new nose was low level gossip; blowing a married man and getting stuck to his crotch was a feast the island would dine on for years. Folks would be telling this story at Maria's wedding some day.

I scanned the church for blonde killers. A quarter of the women were fair-haired, although about two thirds of those had dark roots. From this angle it was hard to tell if I'd seen any of them near Kyria Olga's apartment.

"I see a new face among us this morning," Father Spiros said suddenly in his booming voice, breaking away from the words on the page.

How about that, I wasn't the only interloper.

I looked around to see who that might be.

The whole congregation was looking back at me.

Kyria Olga's ghost burst out laughing. "Oh, you are so lucky. So very lucky. I would love to be you right now."

"Little Aliki Callas," Kyria Sofia said. She was in her Sunday finest complete with white wrist length gloves and a white leather-bound bible clasped in her hands. "You were Kyria Olga's friend. You must be here to pray for Olga's soul. Or maybe you think one of us killed her." She sounded cocky. She was right and she knew it, the old fake.

Kyria Olga floated over to Kyria Sofia. She inspected the priest's sister closely, then disappeared behind her. Two ghostly fingers popped out of Kyria Sofia's temples.

"I knew she was Satan's offspring all along," Kyria Olga called out to me.

I counted to ten. Dead Olga Marouli was funnier than living Olga Marouli. Invisibility and lack of consequences do that to a person.

"Welcome, Aliki Callas. Whatever your reason for being with us today, we hope you will join us again in the future," the priest said.

And on that note, the service ended.

The congregation stampeded. They had places to go, people to talk about. A few stragglers remained behind, standing in loose bunches on the church's grounds.

Kyria Sofia linked her arm with mine and steered me towards a shady patch under a fig tree.

Ask me anything," she volunteered cheerfully. "I know everyone and everything in this congregation. Nothing happens that I don't hear about it. People think of me as their closest friend. I want you to do the same, Allie."

Uh huh. I believed her. Really, I did.

Kyria Olga was nearby, hovering over Father Spiros's shoulder. Good, that would keep her from cracking me up. But first, it was time for a little well-placed—although not heart-felt—sycophancy.

"Thank you, Kyria Sofia. I knew you would be the person to speak to. Your reputation as one of Merope's most generous people is well-deserved."

Her smile said *lamb* but her eyes said *wolf*.

She patted my arm. "It is always nice to know one's work in the community is appreciated."

"It is. And I know Kyria Olga would appreciate any help you can give me."

"Anything I can do. *Anything*."

I spread the honey thicker. "I guess it would be too easy to ask if you know anyone who might have had a reason to murder Kyria Olga?"

She raised a gloved hand to her neck and adjusted the

ladybug brooch fastened to the lapel of her cream jacket. "No. If I did I would have given the police that information. Olga was a good, although sometimes brusque, woman. But murder? No. I can't imagine why anyone who knew her would want to hurt her. Certainly no one in our congregation."

I smiled again. "I thought as much. I have to confess while Kyria Olga and I were very good friends, I know little about her social life. I do know she is--was--very lucky at Bingo. Do you play?"

A dark cloud drifted across Kyria Sofia's faux-happy face. "I never gamble."

"They don't play for money."

"Money or prizes, it is all the same abomination in the eyes of God."

My eyes cut to Kyria Olga. She was still sniffing around the priest. I did a double-take. Father Spiros was having a loud, hand-waving conversation with Stavros Psaris, the man who I believed was in love with Kyria Olga.

Kyria Sofia's head swiveled. Her eyes touched on Stavros then darted back to meet mine. "Stavros Psaris," she said in a conspiratorial whisper. "He and Olga's husband were best friends. He must be taking this very hard, the poor man. They were close, you know. He spent a lot of time in her apartment."

The potential scandal hung there. All it needed was Kyria Sofia's mouth to make it go BOOM.

"They were just friends," I said, throwing a thimble of water on the spark.

"Of course they were."

"That's *all* they were."

"I never said they were not. Stavros is a good man. His life has been very sad. His wife died, you know, and then his best friend, and now his best friend's wife. And many years ago he and his wife also lost their son in a war. I do not remember which one ..."

"What happened to his wife?"

If Kyria Olga had mentioned it at some point, I'd forgotten.

"The autopsy was inconclusive. Or so I heard. Irini got sick and the doctors never did figure out what was wrong. She had all the tests ... but nothing. She was pale and drawn for so long, and soon she stopped coming to church altogether. Then one day she just stopped breathing. They say she died in her husband's arms."

My eyes focused on Stavros Psaris with renewed interest. Mental note to self: find out the details of his wife's death. Call it morbid curiosity.

Kyria Sofia's mouth was still moving when a blonde woman joined the two men and the ghost of Olga Marouli. She was middle aged and slim. Deportment of a ballerina with a stick up her *kolos*. She smiled at something the priest was saying.

"Kalliope Kefala's daughter," I murmured.

"Eleni never misses a service. Normally Kalliope comes with her, but I did not see her today. There has always been a gentle rivalry between Kalliope and Olga, you know."

"The knitting thing?"

"Oh yes, the Winter Festival. They have a competition for the best entry in each craft. Olga has won many years for knitting."

None of this was news to me. "It's a shame about Kyria Kalliope's. Is it Alzheimer's?"

A cloud moved across Kyria Sofia's face, and disappeared just as quickly. "Eleni never mentioned it, perhaps it is a new diagnosis. I will have to ask her about it."

"Don't," I said quickly.

But Kyria Sofia was already marching over to Eleni Kefala.

Kyria Olga had vanished again, so I walked home, quietly processing what little I had learned today. All was quiet across the hall so I managed to sneak into my apartment unnoticed. Maybe going to church had paid off—this time, anyway. For half an hour I hunched over the keyboard punching in my thoughts before saving and closing the file. My final act was to add a question mark next to Irini Psari's name.

Finders Keepers is easy to run in this day and age. Technology and the internet can shave a lot leg time off a search. A few keystrokes into Google and I was looking at Irini Psari's obituary. She had passed in 2007, age sixty-two on the day of her death. The obituary confirmed that she and her husband had one son who was killed in Macedonia (not the real Macedonia in Greece, but the wannabe in what used to be Yugoslavia), who would be welcoming his mother into heaven. Strictly sentimental, it was skimpy on details.

Stavros Psaris had seen more than his fair share of heartache. Was anything worse than losing a child?

He didn't kill Olga, I knew it, but I wanted to speak to him anyway. My afternoon was completely free of social obligations. Perfect timing to pay Stavros Psaris a visit.

I took care of business first.

I clicked the little envelope on my desktop and shot off an email to Jimmy Kontos, resident little person, telling him about an upcoming speed-dating meeting at Merope's Best. If that didn't work out, there was a singles mixer coming up. I thought about messing with the guy but decided it was just wrong.

I can be sarcastic and caustic, but I'm not a monster.

Besides, what if he really was a leprechaun?

CHAPTER ELEVEN

Stavros Psaris lived in a sedate bungalow just a few roughly cobbled together blocks away from my apartment. I decided to walk and suck in some fresh air.

Exercise and I are not pals. I don't run anywhere with enthusiasm unless the magic words "chocolate buffet" are mentioned, and the thought of lifting weights makes me want to lie down and take a nap. So aside from riding my bicycle, I get my daily exercise in other more subtle ways. With a walk to get groceries, followed by a jog up two flights of stairs, I could lie to myself and pretend that I wasn't really working out. It's really quite cunning.

I changed back into jeans and kept the black sweater, lacing up boots comfortable enough to walk in, before heading out the door. Dark glasses hid most of my face from the outside world. I wasn't looking forward to winter. It was too difficult to maintain optimum body temperature scrunched down in an alley if a client wanted someone followed. There were only a few weeks left before I'd need gloves and a coat if I didn't want to become a meatsicle on the job.

The putt-putt of a car engine slowed and began to crawl along the narrow street. It pulled up level with me. I peered into the black car--sideways of course—just in case it was some creep, wanting me to show him my breasts.

Leo Samaras was at the wheel, so now I was conflicted: did he want to see my boobs or not? Because probably I wouldn't mind if he did.

He stopped and rolled the window down. "You need a ride?"

I flexed and released my butt cheeks. Pretty firm-ish. I'd already scored one block of exercise, did I really need more? I didn't want to overdo it.

"My mother said not to take rides from strangers."

He grinned. "I'm a police officer, you're quite safe with me."

Oh boy, we were almost flirting again. "Do you have sweets? Because I really can't get in if you have sweets."

"No sweets."

"Okay. But no funny business or I'll bite."

"Tease." There he went again with the panty-remover smile.

He waited until I buckled the seatbelt before pulling away from the curb. Good policeman.

"Where are you going?"

"Why?"

"I have to know where to take you."

Oh. Right.

I coughed up the directions. People around the island navigated more by landmark than address.

"Stavros Psaris's place?"

I glanced over, surprised. "You know him?"

"I know his name."

"Is that right?"

"Small island. Whispers about wife who dies of a mysterious illness. We're looking closely at everyone involved. It wasn't difficult to get a look at the old records."

"And?"

"Nothing. His wife died of leukemia. It's well documented. They kept it quiet, that's all. Kyrios Psaris lived a clean life, and he wasn't responsible for his wife's death. Not unless he can give people cancer."

Take that, Kyria Sofia.

I looked over at him. "So you've checked him out already for this thoroughly?"

He answered with a crooked half smile. "Yeah. He didn't have an alibi, but I don't think he's our man."

I nodded. To be fair I wasn't just going over there to try to clear him of a crime. The carefully concealed romantic bones in my body wanted to discover more about Stavros Psaris's unrequited love for Kyria Olga. Maybe I was just hankering after a genuine love story. It had been a while since I'd had a glimpse of the real thing. I wasn't even sure that I believed in love and happy-ever-after. Not anymore.

"So where are you going?" I asked him.

"To see Stavros Psaris."

I swiveled in the bucket seat and glared in his face. "No, you're not."

"I am. Running into you was a coincidence. Honest."

His mouth twitched. Liar.

I flopped back in the seat and stared at the road ahead. This time last week I'd only seen Leo maybe once or twice, and then only in the distance. Now he seemed to be everywhere.

"So did Dimitri and Maria finally come apart?"

Leo snorted. "It took that whole bottle of solvent."

"So what's the damage?"

"Glue burns, but they're both going to be fine. Dimitri got the worst of it."

"Total Brazilian?"

"Not a hair left. And his nose is a mess."

"I guess that punch spells doom for those lovebirds. So you're going to tag along?"

"And see you in action? Wouldn't miss it."

The man had a smart mouth on him; I liked that. Maybe we could be friends.

Maybe you want more, the little voice inside me said.

Maybe I did.

———

Like most houses on Merope, Stavros Psaris's house was a single layer of white stucco. The roof was red tile and the shutters were blue. He had a garden in red pots, but it was hunkering down for the inevitable winter.

Stavros Psaris opened the door with the lethargy of a man who had made peace with constant grief. "Detective." He nodded, then his eyes slid over to me and he smiled all the way to his warm brown eyes. "Allie, it is a pleasure to see you again. Come in. I just put the coffee on."

He shuffled back into the house and we followed.

If I'd expected the stodgy home of an old man, I was wrong. Stavros Psaris's home was light and airy, although small. Every little thing was tasteful, down to the ornaments in a cherry cabinet in the living room. Above the fireplace, a beautiful woman of forty or so looked down on me. She was exotic in oils, her hair dark, eyes filled with immense kindness and a hint of sadness. I wondered if this was the late Irini Psaris, and if so, was I projecting the sadness upon the woman because I knew of their tragic loss? I stared at the portrait a little longer trying to decide.

"Beautiful, Yes?" Our host didn't wait for an answer. "That is my Irini. She agreed to sit for me during my forty-fifth summer. I'd been at her for years to be my subject. Finally I had to bribe her, telling her it was all I wanted for my birthday."

"You painted this?" My words were soft and reverent in the face of so much talent and beauty. For a moment I envied the late Irini Psari; she was loved so much that he begged to capture her on canvas.

"That I did." He turned to Leo, who was discretely looking about the room, his cop eyes casually watchful. "You two ready for some coffee?"

We both said, "Please."

"Do you need some help?" I offered. I've never felt entirely comfortable with anyone waiting on me.

The older man waved me away. "Sit, sit. I do not get much company, and I feel we might have a long talk ahead of us." He shuffled off, presumably to the kitchen.

Leo was staring at me.

"What?"

"Did you see the photographs?"

I looked around seeing what he saw for the first time. Upon entering the room I'd been so transfixed on the painting that everything else went largely unnoticed. Now all the details came into focus, and the photographs in their heavy silver frames surfaced. In some of the photographs the face of a smiling boy with tousled hair and a sprinkling of freckles looked back at me. As my eyes took in each new picture, the boy grew, until soon he was a young man, tousled curls gone and replaced with a shaved scalp. It must have captured him just before he went to Macedonia.

The rest of the photographs were testament to the life of Irini Psari. Each pose was different, yet in each one she wore the same sweet smile of a woman who was a far better person than I'd ever be.

My hand reached out and picked up one of the frames. It felt heavy and warm in my hand. "It's a shrine," I said quietly.

"A shrine to true love," Leo whispered from behind me. He was standing so close I could feel his warm breath brush my cheek as he spoke.

I forced myself to stand still. If I turned around now, I'd end up kissing him, I could feel it.

I swallowed slowly.

A soft clinking broke the spell. Leo moved away. Suddenly the air around me felt cold, empty. Stavros Psaris was back carrying a tray with three demitasse cups and three tall glasses of water

"Drink up. It will put hair on your chests." He indicated for us to sit. He took the easy chair. I perched on the edge of the couch, trying not to notice that Leo's leg was a hair away from mine.

"Even now I cannot believe she is gone," Kyrios Psari said.

Which woman?

He answered my question with his next breath.

"Irini is ... was ... the love of my life, and the mother of our only child." His voice crackled. "It nearly killed me when he died. Then when Irini went, I wanted to die with her. There was not a minute of the day that I did not pray for it. But thanks to Stathis and Olga, I survived. I say survived because I only did what was necessary to keep drawing breath. The pain prevented me from really living. All I did was work, eat, and sometimes sleep."

"What changed?" Leo asked. He was leaning forward, listening, observing, always the cop.

Stavros laughed. It wasn't the sound of mirth, more like thinly concealed pain. "Who says anything changed? I still miss her every moment of every day. But I go on breathing in and out every day." His hands shook as he spooned more sugar into the cup. "And now Olga is gone too."

"You loved her." I realized my body language had shifted to mimic Leo's. I hunched forward, elbows resting on my knees while I sipped at the hot coffee.

"I did. But not as I loved Irini. Great love only comes once, and do not let anyone tell you otherwise." He settled back into the sofa cushion. "When Stathis died, Olga and I were both alone. I had always thought her to be beautiful, even when we were all young and raising families. But my admiration was always distant. I was too much in love with Irini to really notice another woman, you understand. I comforted Olga as she and Stathis had comforted me. We went to church together, and I played bingo, even though I do not like it, just to keep her company. Maybe I did it for myself as much as for her. We both became a little less lonely over time, and the one day I woke up and realized I looked forward to seeing her and that funny purple hair."

"She'd argue that it was lilac," I said.

This time there was some humor in his laugh. "That was Olga for you. I am a simple man—what do I know about fancy colors? To me it was purple. She was Irini's opposite in so many ways. I think that's why they were so close. But they both had that core of kindness within them. Maybe I loved Olga because she was all that was left of my Irini. But, I would like to believe it was more than that." He closed his eyes for a moment and when he opened them I saw what he had been hiding, even from himself, until now. "Guilt. It chipped away at me every single day after I began to love Olga. Guilt because I loved another. In my mind, it tarnished my love for Irini, made my love for her less important. I have borne that burden, and now both women are gone and I am alone once again."

I reached across the table and took his hand. "Kyria Olga

cared for you very much. It's so rare to find real love. You've been fortunate, You found it twice."

"You are a good girl, Allie." He squeezed my hand. "Olga loved you like a daughter. Her children ... none of them have a shred of their parents' decency."

"I know what you mean," I said.

"They're not that bad," Leo said. But the twitching on his face said otherwise.

"You can't even say that with a straight face," I said.

Stavros Psaris slapped his knee. "I see both of you have enjoyed Athena's company."

"If *enjoyed* means having my entrails pulled out through my nose and sprinkled with cayenne pepper, then yes. She's staying Olga's apartment. They all are."

He looked startled. "Really?"

"Believe me," I said. "I wouldn't lie about something that awful."

"Is something wrong, Kyrios Psaris?" Leo asked.

The old man shook his head. "No, no. I just have a feeling they will be in for a surprise when they see their Olga's will."

"She discussed it with you?"

"Discussed? No, I guess there are some things you two do not know. I am ... *was* Olga's attorney. Let me tell you this: Athena, Tina, and George are going to shit their donkeys."

CHAPTER TWELVE

"Does the will say anything about flogging them?" I asked, perhaps a little too eagerly.

He smiled. "No. And I cannot discuss any of the details. All will be revealed in due time."

The funeral was tomorrow, which meant that afterwards the clan would be braying and whinnying until the will was read. I was going to steer well clear of them, although it might have been nice to be a little black fly on the wall with a video camera.

"Olga requested that you be there for the reading of her will," Kyrios Psaris continued.

I looked up, surprised. "But I'm not family."

"So what? I think you will find it is in your best interest to be there. 4:00 P.M. at my old office."

I blinked, still not really comprehending. Surely I couldn't be entitled to anything Olga Marouli owned. Perhaps she wanted to give a me some small token to remember her by, like a sweater or knitting needles.

"I'll be there."

Leo leaned forward with the thoughtful expression on his

face again. Obviously he still had some questions. "To your knowledge, did Olga Marouli have any enemies?"

Stavros leaned back and closed his eyes for a moment. "She had a sharp tongue so it is possible she offended somebody. But enemies? No."

"How well do you know Eleni Kefala?" I asked, thinking she was one of the few blondes in Kyria Olga's extended circle.

This time the old man chuckled. "I saw you there this morning but I didn't want to intrude on whatever you had going with Sofia. Eleni is a good woman. Not warm, but good. She and my boy were a couple, many years ago. Irini and I hoped that they would be married when he came back, but it was not meant to be. She still checks in on me now and again."

"I spoke to her mother yesterday. Does she have memory problems?"

"Memory problems?"

I explained how she'd faded out during our conversation at the knitting circle.

He looked shocked. "I had no idea. Kalliope has always been spirited woman. She and Olga have been subtle rivals for years with their crafts. And in the bingo hall."

"She plays bingo too?"

He grinned. "You should have seen her face whenever Olga won the big prizes."

"Sounds like she was always coming second place," I said.

"I think they both thrived on their competition. I doubt either of them would have had it any other way." His chuckle gave way to a lung-busting cough.

Leo stood. "We should get going."

I waited until the older man stopped coughing. "You'll be at the funeral tomorrow?"

Kyrios Stavros cleared his throat and wiped tears from his

eyes with a large blue handkerchief—the manly type with a broad stripe around the edges. "I will be there. There is to be no wake, I understand. Olga wanted it that way."

"Her children wanted a wake, and they wanted to have it at my place."

"What?"

"You know Athena," I said. "She hasn't mentioned it since I just about popped a major blood vessel."

"That woman ..." He shook his head. "I will see you tomorrow. I would not miss the chance to say goodbye to my friend."

I liked this man. He was warm and kind.

Leo and Kyrios Stavros shook hands. I reached up and pecked him on the cheek. He beamed back down at me.

"Come see me sometime," he said. "Both of you."

When we got back to his car, Leo held the door open for me. Stavros Psaris was still in his doorway, waving. It felt good, like something a grandparent would do.

The air began to shift around him, and for a moment the figure of a slender dark-haired woman appeared to his left. I recognized Irini Psari instantly. Stavros Psaris's true love was still with him, even in death.

"You're a kind woman," Leo said as he clicked his seatbelt.

My eyebrows took a hike to higher ground. "I can provide references to the contrary." I checked my phone. One lonely text from Toula requesting that I come over for lunch today.

I made a face. I'm not a fan of lunch served with lectures or peppered with disapproving glances.

"Something wrong?"

"Not really."

"Animal, vegetable, or mineral?"

I was never going to live our first meeting down. "Vegetable, I think. It's my sister."

"Toula?"

I twisted around to look at him. "You know Toula?"

His lips twitched. "You really don't remember me do you?"

"What's that supposed to mean?"

"I used to come to your house."

A chill settled in my belly. "When?" My parents still lived in my childhood home, when they weren't floating around the world in a luxury coffin. I had no recollection of Leo Samaras in my parents' house at any time during my teen years. And believe me, I'd remember.

"It's true. I used to get a kick out of that little frog that used to croak when someone approached the front door."

He was telling the truth, there was a frog. In fact it was still there to this day croaking every time someone rang the doorbell. Frantic mental scrambling took place in my brain as I tried to recall how and when he'd been in my house.

"You and Toula were friends?"

"Something like that."

I rummaged around in my memory.

"You used to date my sister!"

It came out accusatory and hostile. I was acting about as mature as your average fourteen-year old.

He grinned. "I did. But I didn't inhale."

I wasn't laughing. "You dated my sister."

"Briefly."

"For most of her junior and all of her senior year!" I glared at him. "You look different."

He did look different. Back then Leo Samaras had been beanpole thin. As I recalled, he'd had scruffy long hair that came dangerously close to being a mullet. There were none of the lean hard muscles he had now, and his broad shoulders were narrow and thin. Back in those days, Leo always wore a black t-shirt with some metal band like Def Leppard or Metallica printed on front and black jeans.

No wonder I didn't recognize him. He was a whole new person, and so ... clean.

He and Toula used to lock themselves in her room while our parents were at work. I had to be home when Toula's boyfriend came around because good Greek girls don't hang out at home alone with boys. I was all that stood between my sister and a reputation assassination.

"You made some changes yourself. How is Toula?" His eyes fixed on the road ahead, but his lips twitched now and again revealing his amusement at my barely concealed distress.

"Aside from her recent exile from Uranus and her insatiable need to ridicule my life choices, she's fine. Why? Are you still interested?"

He chuckled. "You used to be such a cute kid. When did you get so sarcastic?"

A snort popped out of my nose before I could stop it. "I can't take you seriously now that I know you used to make out with my sister. To do so would be turning against years of prejudice and sibling rivalry, and I'm too set in my convictions, no matter how silly you might find them."

"Who said I find them silly?"

He stopped outside our apartment building.

"I'm being preemptive. I can't believe I liked you. You dated my *sister*."

"You like me?"

Out of the corner of my eye I could see him grinning.

With a click I unbuckled the belt and reached down to grab my bag. "Liked—past tense. I couldn't possibly like anyone that Toula ever swapped spit with. It would be a gross display of poor judgment. And it's a pity because you are really attractive even though I saw you playing human octopus with that woman the other night." I shut my eyes for a moment. "God, you smell *good*. That's not fair. Stop smelling so good." I climbed out of the car and peered in through the open door. "And in case you think I'm a total ingrate, I'm not, I really do appreciate the ride. So, thank you." I swiveled on one heel and stalked toward the apartment complex door.

I saw his reflection in the glass door. He looked puzzled, as though I'd just smacked him around the head with a two-by-four and he couldn't quite figure out what happened.

"At least kiss him goodnight," Yiannis the former gardener said from his spot in the bushes.

"What would you know?" I asked. "You're dead!" With a loud huff, I yanked the door handle and left Leo Samaras behind.

———

On my way inside I stopped in the lobby. With everything that had been going on I had neglected to check my mail. I located the small brass key on my key ring and slid it into the lock. The metal door popped open, its contents spilling out into my arms. Bills, junk mail, more junk, and a thick package with my name printed on front in a flowery hand. It had the heft of a brick and was sent from here on Merope.

Although I love to protest that I hate packages and presents on my birthday, deep down I feel like an excited kid when gifts show up.

But it wasn't my birthday.

And I hadn't ordered anything.

This was a mystery package.

I carried it carefully upstairs in case it was a mail bomb, slid it onto the coffee table and weighed my options. I could open it and—BOOM! My life would be over, bits of me splattered on the walls. Or I could just leave it on the table collecting dust, like all my other knick knacks.

I poured a glass of water and eyed the package.

Surely it wouldn't hurt to sniff it?

I leaned forward. Inhaled. A powdery sweetness tickled my nose. If it was a mail bomb, someone had gone to the trouble of concealing it inside a cake.

Was that a loose edge? I *hate* loose edges.

With one fingernail I picked at the offending paper. A long strip tore free, leaving me with a half-covered box. The smell of baked goods was stronger now.

Either I'd get blown to bits or I wouldn't. If I survived, I'd get to eat whatever was inside the box.

The remaining paper fell away easily, and nestled inside was a box identical to the one I'd tossed in the trash that morning. Cake Emporium was stenciled in gold on top of the royal blue box.

Today was my lucky day. I should buy a Greek Lotto ticket.

Stuck to the side was a small envelope. The note inside read, Dearest Allie, please accept our gift. Come see us again soon. Toodles, Betty and Jack.

Nestled inside were half a dozen cupcakes, just like the ones I'd finished this morning. I plucked one out. It looked innocent enough, and it wasn't like I was taking baked goods from a complete stranger. Betty wasn't likely to get any repeat business from me if she killed me now, was she?

Feeling better already, I finished the cupcake while I ran a hot bath. If I had to spend the afternoon with Toula and her clan, I'd have to stock up on peace of mind.

———

I showered on autopilot. My mind was busy dealing with the Leo situation.

We'd had chemistry, and now we had nothing.

Toula and Leo? *Really?*

Irritation weaved its insidious way through my thoughts. I'd reacted like a brat instead of a grown woman. First I'd snarled at Leo, then I followed it up by berating him for someone he did when was seventeen. The bitter icing on the cake was that I'd stomped off without giving him a chance to speak. And I had no defense, except that I was more attracted to Leo than I wanted to be.

The last time I cared about a man he left.

Forever.

The water cooled faster than normal. Or I'd been in here longer than I expected. If I didn't start getting ready now, Toula would probably poison my food. I threw on a black sweater and jeans and shoved my feet into boots. Then I took a few moments to add what little I'd learned today into Kyria Olga's file.

After hearing Kyrios Stavros's opinions about Olga's children, I was afraid I might have to speak to each of her children one by one. Was it possible that one of them knew about her will and killed her out or spite or anger? Leo said they were clean, but how sure was he? Parricide wasn't a new thing. Greek mythology started the trend in Greece when Cronus killed Uranus. Everyone else ran with it after that.

Maybe it was one of the grandkids. Lydia was still unaccounted for.

If Olga had enemies, I sure was missing something. A lifelong petty rivalry with a potentially ill woman didn't count; and it was clear that Stavros Psaris wasn't a killer.

The phone's ear piercing shrill snapped me back to reality.

"I just know he is a cheating *kolotripas!*" Angela Zoubloulaki wailed before I had a chance to speak. Most people don't call the men they love assholes, but Angela was an asshole magnet, so it's possible she was correct.

"Angela, what are you doing?"

"He's cheating," she said with a half sob. "And I have proof. Can you come over?"

If she had proof, why did she need me?

I glanced at my watch. I had thirty minutes before Toula expected me for lunch. "I'll be there in five minutes," I told her.

.

CHAPTER THIRTEEN

Angela lives in a mansion. Big. White. Lots of glass and chrome and geometric fountains. The whole modern confection has a million-euro view from its perch on one of Merope's oceanfront cliffs. And despite the fact that my client employs a small staff so she doesn't have to deal with the myriad little problems that come with owning a huge house, today she yanked open the front door herself. Her eyes were red; her makeup was perfect. Clearly she had her own sorcerer stashed away somewhere.

"My whole life is *skata*!" She grabbed my arm and dragged me into her hermetically sealed white house. Kitten heels clipped and slapped as she led me to her parlor. I'd been in this room a dozen times, and each time it looked different. The most recent redecoration incorporated modern art and uncomfortable white furniture from somewhere Nordic.

Angela wiped at her eyes and sat. She's a plain woman elevated to fabulousness by her wealth and pretty packaging. I like her despite her constant man problems and her neuroses. According to the rumor mill, she had grown up poor on the island of Skopelos. Two marriages, one divorce, and one heart attack had left her a very wealthy woman. Never in history had money suited a woman more. If the poor girl still lived inside her, she was buried under a mountain of cosmetics.

She clutched her chest. "I know Pavlos is cheating. I can feel it in here."

Here was one of her mountainous (and impossibly perky) implants.

I passed her a fresh white handkerchief from the stack on the white-and-glass coffee table. She dabbed at her eyes with the fresh cotton.

"You said you had proof?"

Angela placed a piece of paper in my hand. "Read it."

I scanned the page. The paper was linen and the writing masculine. It contained a poem addressed to his sweet. A bad poem. But then everything I knew about poetry would fit on a grain of rice.

"I don't see the problem." Beside the fact that the poem stunk.

"It's there! At the top!"

I went over it again. Nothing.

"Help me out," I said.

"Pavlos never calls me his sweet. Never ever!" A fresh round of sobbing began as I stared helplessly down at the simple sheet of paper.

Okay ... "What does he call you?"

Her nose honked into the handkerchief again. "My baby, my doll, my girl, but never his sweet. So you see, there's someone else out there that he does think of as his sweet."

Her proof had no proof in it.

"Look," I said gently. "I can have a friend run a background check on him if that will make you feel better. And then you can decide if you want me to follow him for a while."

The sobbing stopped. "You would do that?"

"I can do it tomorrow."

"Why not today?"

"Family obligations. By the time I'm done I'll need a stiff drink and a solid night's sleep, just to hold off the suicidal tendencies."

"I suppose that's okay."

I glanced at my watch. The torture rack was waiting.

————

"Of course I remember Leo. Why do you care?" Toula was giving me the stink-eye across the table. Someone didn't want me to bring up her old boyfriend in front of her husband Kostas, and their kids, Patra (six) and Milos (eight).

"Did I say I care? I don't care. He's the detective in charge of Kyria Olga's you-know-what."

I didn't want to say *murder* in front of my niece and nephew. They were a precocious pair and bound to ask a million uncomfortable questions. Patra is the world's biggest worrywart, stressing over every tiny thing, from whether or not her next loose tooth would bounce off the roof when she tossed it up there for luck, to whether or not she would catch (and invariably die from) the potential pandemic of the moment. She'd greeted me at the front door, hysterical about some billion-year-old virus scientists had dug up in Antarctica.

They're cute kids who looked more like Kostas, with his light brown eyes and his reddish brown hair, than Toula; although Milos has his mother's nose.

"I heard he was back on the island."

"I never thought skinny Leo with his Metallica t-shirts would end up fighting crime," I said.

"Does he ... do *they* have any idea who did that thing that happened yet?" She forked a chunk of lamb into her mouth.

"Who did what, Mama?" Milo's eyes were alert, fork in one hand, bread in the other.

"Don't worry. It is nothing," Kostas said. His thin shoulders were hunched as he shoveled a small stack of feta and olives into his mouth. Mostly he ignores Toula and me when we talk. It's safer than way. Kostas owns Go Car Go, an automotive repair shop. Even when he's just showered he smells like engine oil.

"Why would he worry about it if it's nothing?" Patra piped in.

I answered my sister's question. "No."

"Mommy, what's a virgin?" Milos wanted to know.

Kostas sighed into his food.

"A woman who hasn't had a baby," my sister said automatically.

"Like Thea Allie?" he said.

Toula turned red. Not me. I grinned at my nephew and said, "Definitely."

"Who is Leo?" Patra wanted to know. "Was he your boyfriend, Mama?"

"He was a friend of the family," Toula lied.

Patra wasn't done with her line of questioning. "Has Leo had a baby? Or is he a virgin, too?"

"I guess he's a virgin, too," I said. "How's school?"

"I'm going to be a movie star," Patra said.

Her brother flicked breadcrumbs at her. "No one will pay to see you."

"Will too."

"Won't."

"Mama!"

"Stop it, you two," Toula said, on autopilot.

I was curious. "What kind of movie star? Action? Comedy?"

"I want to be one that dances naked and orders lots of pizza. Baba's movies always start with pizza. I really love pizza."

I didn't make eye contact. With anyone. Probably I never would again.

Toula vanished into the kitchen. She came out with a bottle of ouzo and poured herself a good five centimeters. One gulp later it was gone.

Kostas went right on eating.

I contemplated birth control choices, just in case I ever had sex again.

After lunch, Kostas plonked himself down in front of the television and the kids raced outside to play. Toula and I were on clean-up duty.

"Why did you lie about Leo?"

Toula snapped a pair of rubber gloves on and ran hot water in the sink. "Who lied? Not me. We were all friends."

"I wasn't his friend. I was his girlfriend's little sister."

"It was so long ago—who remembers?"

Wow, someone was seriously in denial, and I was sure it wasn't me. "He asked about you."

Something flickered in her eyes. "I doubt that. What is he doing?"

"Besides being a policeman? He lives above me. Directly above me."

"I didn't know you knew him so well."

"We just met—well, re-met—Friday night. He looks different now. I didn't recognize him."

"Different how?"

"Tall. Fit. Gorgeous."

"You're not—"

"No."

Her face relaxed. "And you won't ..."

"I don't need your leftovers."

Cruel, yes, but I felt I owed her that for making the first decent man I'd met in ages immediately off-limits. It was a screwed-up principle, but I couldn't help myself.

Toula flinched.

I looked away.

"Hey, Toula," Kostas yelled from the living room. "Bring me a beer."

"Get it yourself," she yelled back.

There was a long pause. Then:

"Is it that time of the month already?"

Toula grabbed a beer from the refrigerator, twisted the lid off, spat into the bottle. Then she handed it to me. "He wants a beer, he gets a beer."

———

Kyria Olga's kids were watching television.

Good. That meant I could sneak through my door without waking the kraken.

My brain was full and my calendar was empty, which meant it was work o'clock.

Bundled in soft flannel pajamas, I poured a glass of water and grabbed a cupcake from the box. I took a sip and a bite, and carried both over to my desk. I shot off an email to my old boss with all the information about Pavlos Mavros that Angela had given me. Background checks were Sam's thing. He could find a grain of dirt in a sandpit.

I rocked slowly in the chair and stared at the screen. For Angela's sake, I hoped Pavlos had no secrets to hide. It would be difficult enough to convince her that he was sincere, even when all possibilities were exhausted. Sometimes—no, most of the time—I suspected Angela thrived on drama and purposely embarked on a series of affairs with morally ambiguous men to get her fix.

An addiction like any other.

Sam emailed me back almost instantly with the basics. He promised to dig a little deeper to see what was hiding beneath the public layers. With one click I was poking into the deep, not-so-dark crevices of Pavlos Mavros's life. No criminal record. A bankruptcy four years earlier, two current credit cards, with a total credit line of three-thousand euros, and one savings account at national bank, with a balance of five-hundred euros and twenty-three cents.

Well now, this was interesting. I leaned forward, elbows either side of the keyboard. The letters came into sharper focus. I wasn't imagining things. Pavlos Mavros was currently employed at Go Car Go, which meant his boss was Kostas, my brother-in-law.

CHAPTER FOURTEEN

The morning of Olga Marouli's funeral, I woke before the local roosters started nagging me. The clock read 5:21 A.M.

I was glad to be awake.

All night long, yesterday's events blended into a demented nightmare stew designed to give even the sanest person the creeps. As if recent events hadn't already made me question my sanity.

Still thinking about Pavlos Mavros and his connection to my brother-in-law, I staggered into the kitchen for water. As I finished the last drop, the familiar shimmer that heralded the arrival of Olga Marouli's spirit materialized. I noticed right away that her outfit was different: a neat black suit trimmed with fox fur. Like a classy dame from a 1940s black and white movie, except old and stooped.

"Nice outfit." I refilled the glass from the kitchen faucet.

She twirled mid-air. "Do you like it? I borrowed it from Joan Crawford."

"Joan Crawford? I guess you didn't find it hanging on a wire coat hanger then."

Kyria Olga huffed. "She is not so bad. Although she was a bit bold asking me for a kiss in return."

Everything had a price, even in the afterlife. "Did you kiss her?"

"Of course not! I am still faithful to my husband. But I did think about it."

"Were all your loved ones there, you know, when you ... died?"

She cackled. "My Virgin Mary, I always loved your sense of humor. You could say my arrival was unscheduled, so everyone was busy. Stathis was playing golf, and my mother was busy taking harp lessons from a scantily clad Bulgarian."

"I had coffee with an old friend of yours yesterday. Stavros Psaris.

"Oh?" Her fingers fiddled with the dead fox around her neck.

"It's a shame about his wife and son. He's seen a lot of grief."

"That he has." Her eyes glazed over with nostalgia. "Irini was my best friend. We saw a lot of good times together; bad ones too. But when their son died ... that was the worst. It might have broken them completely if they had not loved each other so much. Thanassi was such a good boy. We had hopes for a while that he and Athena might have unprotected sex and end up having to get married."

Poor guy. Who'd wish that on him?

My old friend hovered just a hair over the easy chair, both hands folded primly on her black tweed lap. A demure twist of the ankles completed the picture of royal elegance.

"Will you be at my funeral?" she asked.

Clink! The empty glass touched metal in the sink. "Of course. Wouldn't miss it for the world."

"Is that what you're wearing?"

I looked down at my pajamas. "I thought I might add

some fluffy bunny slippers and put my hair in some of those pink foam curlers. Heck, I might even spring for a hairnet."

She made a tutting noise. "You will never get a husband if you dress like that. What will your sexy detective think?"

"Same thing he thinks now—that I'm crazy. I know time seems to be on a different schedule in the Great Hereafter, but it's only five-thirty in the morning here on planet Normal. I think I'm entitled to slop-out in my own home at this indecent hour."

"You could buy some of those lacy *sovraka*. I hear men go crazy over the ones with the string that goes right up your *kolos*. If I were younger ..."

"You mean if you were alive?"

"*Po-po*, there you go with the doom and gloom again."

I felt the one-two sucker punch of elation followed by despair as I remembered that Leo Samaras was my sister's past and therefore not my future.

"He's a great guy, but he's not for me."

"Why not? He is attractive, you are attractive; he is in law enforcement, you like handcuffs; he is single, you are single; he sings in the shower, you sing in the shower—"

My head snapped up. "What do you mean he sings in the shower? Have you been *spying* on him?"

Her eyes cut to the ceiling. "Spying is such an ugly word. We should use a different one."

"You're spying."

"How is that different to what you do?"

The couch springs protested as I flopped down into the plush cushions and closed my eyes. "I get paid." One eye opened a slit. Kyria Olga's lips pursed like a cat's bottom. "A little bird told me Eleni Kefala was Thanassi Psaris's girl-friend and possibly future wife."

Kyria Olga snorted. "Her!"

"You don't like her? She's quite beautiful. How old is she? Fifty?"

"Forty-nine. And she is the same *skata* as her mother."

"Really? Why?"

Pop. She vanished.

I hopped up off the couch and wondered if it might be wise idea to cozy up to Kyria Eleni to see if she would shed some light on Kyria Olga's prejudice—something beyond the knitting and bingo. Also, as one of the few blondes connected with this whole thing, she was on my personal list of potential suspects.

Purposely avoiding the thought of funerals and burials, I dressed in my usual winter uniform of jeans, sweater and boots and rode across the street to Merope's Best. The place was packed. I took my place in line behind Vivi Stamatou— Maria's younger sister—and a friend I didn't recognize. Both were dressed for the pole or for school; I couldn't say for sure which.

I focused my eyes on the menu. Anyone looking at me would think I was trying to decide what to order.

"Please," Vivi said. "If she wasn't such a *putana* she wouldn't be in this position. It's her own fault. But do Mama and Baba see that? No. They're all, 'Don't worry, Maria, we will sue that malakas.'"

"Is it true that her mouth was glued to his *poutsa*?" the other girl asked.

"That's what she gets for giving him a *pipa*. And now she gets new lips, the lucky *skeela*. She gets everything: the new nose, big lips, implants. What do I get? Nothing."

The girls placed their order and moved aside. I ordered my usual, took my coffee, and went out to drink my burnt beans outside.

A black beetle jumped onto the plastic lid. I scooped it up

with a napkin, and shook it onto a planter. It flipped back up into my hair.

Argh!

I waved my arms around, trying to get it out. My hand smacked into something solid. I cringed as a paper cup went sailing over my head and splattered on the sidewalk.

"That was my hot chocolate! I hope you're going to pay for that. And my dry cleaning!"

I knew that voice.

I slowly turned around.

Jimmy Kontos swam into focus. He was standing there in miniature Harley Davidson gear. It would have been cute if I hadn't just knocked his chocolate flying, and if he didn't hate my guts.

I winced. "I'm sorry!"

"I should have known it was you! You planned this, didn't you? You saw me coming out with my hot chocolate, and you said, 'Hey, let me pick on the *nanos* for fun.'"

"I didn't even see you! Are you okay?"

"Of course I'm not okay! It was hot chocolate. H-O-T. Even a big *vlakas* like you has to know what that means. This *skata* isn't exactly tickling my face here."

I offered the napkin in my hand. He snatched it from my fingers and dabbed at his face. When it was soaked he hurled it back at me.

"Hey, that's not nice."

"Neither is beating up a little person."

"I told you it was an accident. I didn't even see you there."

"Why not? Do you need glasses, four eyes?"

"No, it's because you're ..." I waved a hand at him.

"What?"

I shook my head. "Never mind. Can I buy you another one?"

"Yes, you can buy me another one. Then you can shove it

up your huge *kolos!*" He scooped the empty beverage container off the ground and pitched it at me. I jumped aside. The cup landed on the ground with a damp thud.

Jimmy Kontos's middle finger flipped up, then he scurried off.

I stood blinking in the morning sunlight for a moment, wondering what the hell had just happened. Suddenly a massive black truck came whipping around the corner. The brakes squealed as it came straight for me. I jumped. My coffee went flying. My bicycle fell onto road. It went CRUNCH under the truck's tire.

Sitting behind the wheel of the big black truck, Kontos raised his finger again. "Looks like you got a boo-boo, you giant *mouni*." He gunned the truck. The little bastard was gone before I could flip him off.

I dialed the police. Gus Pappas answered.

"Some *nanos* just tried to run me over," I said. "He destroyed my bicycle."

Pappas laughed. "Is that you, Callas?"

"Yes, and I'm trying to do the right thing here."

"Where'd it happen?"

I told him.

"It's private property. There's not much we can do, as long as he wasn't speeding on public roads."

The leprechaun had stepped things up. Fine. This was a game I could definitely play. On the upside, I now had a semi-legitimate reason to visit my brother-in-law at work.

———

I rolled my bicycle into the parking lot at Go Car Go. By the looks of the already-full bays, business was booming for my brother-in-law. His reputation for fixing cars was golden in Merope. Toula mentioned he was trying to lure a regional automotive artist for custom paint jobs. Merope wasn't home to a vast number of cars, but I hoped the artist would come through for my family.

I spotted Pavlos Mavros almost immediately. He was wiping his hands on the rag hanging out of his oil-smudged overalls. I almost didn't recognize him without the drunken gait and a beer in his hand. He dropped the rag and ...

Hello .... Now this was interesting.

Pavlos's long legs carried him across to the end bay where a woman was climbing out of a silver sports car. He embraced her lightly, and although they didn't kiss, there was a definite familiarity between them.

Even from the back, I recognized the impeccable stick-up-butt deportment and the smooth blonde hair of Eleni Kefala.

CHAPTER FIFTEEN

In my line of work you soon learn that a coincidence usually isn't. And right now, knowing that Kyria Eleni and Pavlos were acquainted set off bells and whistles.

Were they lovers?

Other than the initial hug, Kyria Eleni kept a respectable distance. Mind you, I couldn't see her wanting oil all over her pretty red suit.

"They're sleeping together. That's what you're thinking," a masculine voice whispered in my ear.

My battered bicycle hit the ground. I couched down to get it. While I was doing that, I got a good look at the new arrival. He was dead, that much I knew that already. Seeing ghosts doesn't faze me, but I spook easily when anyone sneaks up on me, pulse or no pulse.

Soldier boy was cute in his dress blues and shaved scalp. And young. Because I'd seen his photograph yesterday, I recognized him immediately.

"You're Thanassi Psaris," I said, slightly out of breath.

"*Dekaneas* Thanassi Psaris. Not that it matters now."

Dekaneas. Corporal.

He turned away from me, his gaze focusing on his old sweetheart. "Well, she's not sleeping with him. Used to. But not now. I watch her."

"When was that?"

"All the time."

I shook my head. "No, when were they ..."

"Years ago. He still wants to."

"How do you know?"

"Because I used to be a man."

Inside guy scoop, fair enough. "How do they know each other?" I asked him. "He's newish to Merope, isn't he?"

"Greece is a small country." He looked at me. "Nobody has ever seen me before. How is it that you can see me?"

I shrugged. "It's always been this way, as far back as I can remember."

Thanassi nodded to the mechanic who was still hovering around Eleni. "He's a *skatofatsa*. Isn't that what the kids call it these days?"

Skatofatsa—poopface.

I snorted. "Something like that. And as it happens his current woman suspects the same thing. That's why I'm standing here. Well, that and a broken bicycle."

"I figured you weren't sitting here waiting for a hot date." He glanced over, a hint of playfulness in his eyes. "They met in another car shop years ago. He cut her a deal. Still cutting her deals too."

I wondered how Kostas felt about his employees handing out discounts to pretty faces.

"A deal, huh?"

The soldier vanished.

The deceased aren't too big on the goodbyes.

Speaking of goodbyes, as much as I hated to admit it, I had a funeral to go to.

But first I had to see a man about a bicycle.

———

I dressed slowly. Carefully. I would be saying farewell to my friend, but not goodbye. Not yet.

With a flat hand I smoothed the black skirt over my hips. I'd purchased the severe suit last fall when I needed to attend another funeral—strictly business. Afterwards I'd shoved it to the back of the closet, just in front of the winter coats. It smelled faintly of cedar and lavender mothballs. I should have had it dry cleaned. It was too late now.

"That will do, I suppose," Kyria Olga said while I frowned at my at my reflection in the mirror.

"I'm glad you approve." I turned around and smiled at my old friend. She was still wearing the Joan Crawford suit and fur. "I had a visit from Thanassi Psaris earlier. Nice guy."

"He is a good boy. I thought you would like him." She stared into the mirror and frowned. "That is the worst thing about being dead: no more reflection."

"I thought that was just the undead."

"Oh no, even the really dead do not reflect."

I slung my good black purse over one shoulder then stopped. "Wait, did you have something to do with Thanassi sneaking up on me?"

"Maybe I hinted that you had been helping me ... and that you had met his father. He said he had some information for you. Did you get it?"

I thought back to the conversation. "Other than telling me that he follows Kyria Eleni around, he didn't tell me much. What kind of information?"

She shook her head. "It was none of my business. You are the one who is good at getting information out of people."

I let that slide. "Are you going to walk with me?"

"Not today, my doll. I must check in on my children. I will see you there."

"Try to be discreet," I said. "I don't want people to think I'm talking to myself."

"Relax, they already think you are missing a few eggs from your basket."

She pecked me on the cheek. A cool breath of air touched my skin.

"I will see you there," she said.

I watched the clock.

And waited.

―――――

Like a lot of people, Kyria Olga was even more popular in death than in life. Half the arriving crowd at Ayios Konstantinos were there so they could say they'd attended a murder victim's funeral. We like to pretend we're civilized, but human nature is primal. There's something about murder that attracts the crazies and lookie-loos. Instead of joining the other mourners, I stood off to one side and tried to blend while I waited for the bloodsucking Maroulis kids to appear.

Father Spiros arrived with his sister, Kyria Sofia. She stared right through me as though I was air. How unsurprising.

Someone tapped my shoulder. I jumped and turned, almost tripping in the process. A hand steadied me. I looked up into the face of Leo Samaras.

Of course he was here. This was his case and it was still unsolved. These were his hunting grounds. My eyes lifted and locked with his. He smiled. I felt my own lips curve upwards, matching his.

The world dissolved in a puddle around us. We were alone. There was no funeral, no crowd, no ghost of his relationship with my sister wedged between us.

His hand loosened and dropped away and the world came rushing back with a *whoosh*. The effect made me feel wonky.

"You okay?"

His words cemented me back in the present.

"I'm here, aren't I?"

"Not the same thing."

"Don't. Please."

His eyes hazed over. "Don't what?"

"Don't be too nice to me right now. I'm trying to hold it together. Don't make it more difficult than it already is."

"I can respect that. So," he said, all business, hazel gaze sweeping the arriving mourners. "What do you think? Is our boy or girl here?"

My head swiveled back to blossoming crowd. "I'd bet on it. This is too sensational for a killer to miss. Uh oh ..."

The Marouli offspring arrived with great pomp and fanfare.

In their own minds, anyway.

Athena emerged from the front seat of the taxicab first, the vehicle lurching in her significant wake. Mismatched shades of black velvet and lace. Slippers on her feet. Stringy hair that hadn't seen shampoo this week.

Her husband Marko was next, in a thrift store suit, accented with a crooked plaid bowtie. My pity for him lasted about as long as it took to remember that he married and stayed with Athena. On purpose. The man had the survival skills of a lemming.

The youngest Marouli grandchild was still dressed in black, metal still firmly attached to his face for the occasion.

Tina gripped her brother George's arm. She stumbled when she lifted one high heeled pump onto the curb. George held her fast and righted her while she remained oblivious to the whole planet. As far as families went, this one was a mess.

The Maroulis trooped into the church, wearing their

various grievances on the sleeves of their mourning clothes. What would become of them once Kyria Olga was in the ground and her will became public knowledge?

Leo's hand cupped my elbow. We stood back until the other mourners entered the church, then he steered me inside.

"Why so far back?" I whispered.

He rapped a knuckle on my head. "The view's better back here."

"Right," I said, a distinct peevishness making itself at home. He was here to work. I was here to put my friend in the ground ... and keep an eye out for trouble. We were supposed to be on separate sides of the church (women to the left; men to the right), but he was ignoring protocol.

The black box containing the empty shell of Olga Marouli was heavy with flowers. None were from me. Not long ago, Olga and I had discussed death, and she was adamant that I wasn't to waste money on flowers. I could hardly stand to look at her casket. My eyes cut over to the stained glass windows, where the apostles looked as miserable as I felt.

Leo closed the gap between us with his hand, and enveloped mine in his. I didn't protest, didn't pull away. I didn't want to. Toula or no Toula, right now I needed him.

Eventually Father Spiros quit his chanting. He stepped aside and George Maroulis took his place and began talking about how much he loved his mother.

I hadn't been asked to speak. Thankfully. If I had to chose between public speaking and being devoured by dinosaurs, I'd take my chances with dinosaurs.

Up front, the rest of the Maroulis were lined up like gloomy skittles. A mournful wailing began as George droned onward. Athena, I just knew it.

I glanced sideways at Leo. His attention was elsewhere. I followed his gaze all the way to Kyria Kalliope and her daugh-

ter, Eleni. The elderly woman was openly weeping. Eleni
Kefala's mouth was a sour curve and the object of her disap-
proval was her mother. What was her problem?

The more I saw of Eleni Kefala, the less I liked her.

"Hard to imagine her young and attached to Thanassi
Psaris," he whispered.

I stared at the two women with their identical hair and
profiles. Only the less firm chin and white hair of the mother
set them apart.

"There's a word for women like Eleni Kefala," I
whispered back.

"Striking?"

I rolled my eyes. Men. "Praying mantis. Are we sure
Thanassi died in combat?"

"Positive," he said. I raised my brows. "No decapitation
killings by oversized insects in the files—I checked."

"You're humoring me," I said.

"Would I do that?"

"Yes."

"I'm offended," Leo said. "I always take murder seriously.
My paycheck relies on it."

Suddenly the church door flew open. Light flooded in,
framing a stunning blonde in too-little dress. She rocked on
one stiletto heel, her hips swaying.

"My Virgin Mary," the blonde said. "So the old woman
really is dead." She scanned the congregation. "So ... which
one of you *malakes* killed her?"

Leo leaned down to whisper in my ear. "Who is *that*?"

I kicked the green monster dancing in my head. I had no
claim on Leo, so it was totally stupid to be even a tiny bit jealous. But I was.

"That, you dog," I whispered, "is the black sheep of the
family."

CHAPTER SIXTEEN

Lydia Marouli entered the church like a violent storm compressed into micro mini dress and spiked heels. Platinum blond hair. Red lips. Lashings of liquid liner and false lashes that made her look like she'd taken a wrong turn at a cover shoot.

My lip drooped down into a pout while Leo continued to stare at her. No doubt about it, she was a knockout.

All heads turned as she shoved her uncle off the stand and grasped the podium. She laughed, big and full and sensual. Every last person in the church was holding their breath, including me.

"I would have been here sooner but I was on Mykonos." She stared down at her nearest relatives. "My Virgin Mary, Thea Athena, you get fatter every time I see you, which is an absolute miracle given how much you talk. How do you find time to eat? And Theo Marko, why don't you just be a man and shove your *poutsa* in her mouth for once? That will make the old donkey *skasmos*. Oh come on, don't look so horrified. You know I'm right. And good old Theo George." She tilted her pretty blond head. "Remember that time you accidentally walked in on me in the shower when I was fourteen? Do you still like to peep at little girls?" She stared down at her pierced cousin. "Better watch out when you start bringing girlfriends home. Mom, ease up on the pills and booze, you pathetic junkie. Don't any of you say a word, I know you're all here to grab what you can. Fucking hypocrites, you make me want to puke."

She stared her family down, daring them to challenge her.

Nobody spoke. They were too busy watching the show.

With a disgusted snort, Lydia pushed herself away from the podium and stormed back out the front doors, heels clicking.

I wrinkled my nose as she strode past. Even her perfume, while not unpleasant, was fierce.

Everyone sat in stunned silence.

We all wanted to see if she was coming back.

Then the buzz began. Heads turned, the whispers steadily climbing the decibels until it became a full-bodied symphony of small-town gossip.

Somewhere up front a deep wail started, like a she-cat in heat. Athena was at it again. She stood and loomed over her sister, fleshy features warped in a carnival-glass reflection, her mouth stretched wide like Edvard Munch's *Scream*.

Even in her prescription-drug haze, Tina cowered, shrinking to half her size inside her dark threads.

The whispering stopped. A howl broke loose from Athena's throat and she rushed toward her mother's casket. She hurled herself at the flower-covered box, crushing the arrangements as she landed spread-eagle on top of them. Lilies and roses died. Fragrance from smothered petals mixed with the already-strong perfume in the air.

I didn't know whether to laugh, weep, or gag. What squeaked out was like a cat forcing up a hairball. Leo squeezed my hand. I wiggled my fingers free and curled them around the strap of my bag. They'd be safe there, less inclined to wander.

Athena continued to howl and rant.

(It's normal—even expected—for women to wail and throw themselves on the casket at the cemetery. Athena's performance was wildly premature.)

Her words were incoherent, muffled against the wood. Father Spiros stood a short distance away, face turned toward Christ, begging the Son for a quick, quiet exit strategy. Nothing like this had ever happened to him before, judging from the bewildered yet exasperated look on his face.

"This is the best day of my life," Kyria Olga said, appearing beside me.

"Shhh ..." I hid the warning under my hand.

"Why? Nobody can hear me except you."

"She's your daughter, can't you do something?"

"And ruin all this?"

I gave her dirty look. Her laughter came to a slamming halt.

"What am I supposed to do? In case you have not noticed, I am suffering from a fatal case of death. All I can do now is laugh."

"Believe me, I noticed." I turned my head so that Leo couldn't see my lips move. "Haven't you learned anything useful in those afterlife orientation classes? Rattle some windows, slam a door, tell a joke, something. Anything."

Her lips pursed. "This is my funeral, not the theater. Anyway, that sort of thing is frowned upon. I really cannot interfere, so I am going to sit back here and enjoy the show. If I had known my funeral would be this much fun I would have brought a little snack."

The crowd had moved beyond speech. People were beginning to laugh. A few were holding up their phones, collecting footage they could cackle over again later. The laughter was infectious. It spread through the crowd, quicker than a plague.

Athena's grief was a lot of things—but funny?

This wasn't okay. Nothing about this was okay.

"Remember how you made me promise this wouldn't become a sideshow carnival? Congratulations, it's a carnival."

Kyria Olga shrugged. "You want to do something about it, go ahead!"

"Talking to yourself?"

I looked up into Leo's eyes. He seemed to be amused.

"Allergies."

"Allergies?"

"Never mind. If no one else is going to do anything about this circus, I guess I'll do it." With a huff, I threw my handbag strap over one shoulder and left the dead Kyria Olga and the very much alive Leo Samaras behind.

I elbowed my way through the gawkers. Athena was flailing, flowers were flying, and she was moaning like a tipped cow. Legs akimbo for traction, I wrapped my arms around her waist, and heaved.

She popped like a cork and stumbled backwards. It was touch and go for a moment as we swayed. I pushed forward and we stabilized.

The noise level dropped again. The laughter died.

Even Athena's family were still, their faces curious. Maybe Athena deserved their contempt. No doubt she'd cajoled, belittled and bullied them, the way she tried to do to me. But she was their family.

I put my arm around Kyria Olga's eldest child and lead her toward the doors. "You're a bunch of ghouls," I snapped. "She just lost her mother. Show some compassion."

So what if I didn't like Athena?

Right now that didn't matter.

She was a human being. My friend's daughter.

———

Athena sobbed all the way home. When I say sobbed, I mean she made a curious hybrid of noises, not unlike a dozen pigs rooting for truffles. It was dreadful, but nothing about grief is pretty.

The wailing continued while I settled her onto my sofa and made coffee.

I carried both cups to the living room, keeping one for myself. I parked my backside in the opposing chair and waited while she sipped.

"Why are you being nice to me?"

"Your mother just died."

She eyed me. "What do you want?"

Wow, the coffee worked fast. Her suspicious nature was already making a comeback.

"Giving isn't always about getting. I thought you might want a chance to pull yourself together before you go to the cemetery."

She responded by pulling a wad of tissues from a pocket and rubbing them across her nose. The fibers gave her mustache its own mustache.

"She did it. I know she did. I would swear upon my mama's life."

This wasn't a diplomatic time to point out that her mother was dead, which was exactly why we were here.

"Who did what?"

"That *putana*! She has never been any good. No wonder Tina hides in a bottle of ouzo and eats more pills than food. And her father—"

"Are you talking about Lydia?"

"Who else would I be talking about? Why are you asking so many questions?"

"You started it," I said.

Athena grunted. My sofa springs squealed as she leaned back into the cushions. "Of course it was her. No one else would want to kill Mama."

"Okay," I said slowly. "Why? Usually murder has a motive."

She buried her nose in the tissue again and blew. "Because she could."

Oh, well, there was solid proof.

Back in the land of sane people, I nodded. "People commit murder for all kinds of reasons: revenge, fun, money ..."

"Money. The *putana* wants Mama's money."

Did Lydia stand to profit from Olga's death? Stavros Psaris's words came back to me, making me wonder if Olga meant to bypass her kids and divide her assets between the grandchildren instead.

I groaned inwardly. Killing for money, it was totally cliché. Where were all the criminals with originality hiding?

Athena wiped at her eyes again. "You got anything to eat around here?"

———

In the end, I skipped Kyria Olga's burial. I wasn't ready to say goodbye. Plus she wasn't *gone* gone anyway. Probably someone professionally qualified would say that I was avoiding reality, but the reality is that death and The End aren't the same thing.

Athena rejoined her family grudgingly.

I didn't wait to watch the graveside reunion. Instead, I stopped at Merope's Best for awful coffee and chewed a hangnail over today's paper, my mind focused on whether Athena was right about her niece's penchant for murder.

Say she was right and Lydia had killed her own grandmother, paving the way for a likely modest windfall ... why now? Financial crisis? Plain old greed?

Was it that cold and easy?

I ordered a second cup of coffee to go. At home I devoured a cupcake, then another. Probably I should go thank Betty for the gift. And if a few more should fall into a box while I was there, it wasn't exactly my fault, was it?

———

"Looks like the giant has to get herself a new bicycle."

I stifled a raised middle finger. I wanted to do it. I *really* did.

Jimmy Kontos was standing outside my apartment building, a whole meter from where Yiannis the dead gardener was inspecting the bushes.

"Willy Wonka called. He wants you back at the chocolate factory," I said.

His eyes narrowed. "Did you just call me an Oompa Loompa?"

"If the tiny white overalls fit ..."

"I'm gonna kick your *kolos*!"

"Tell you what, I'll wait right here while you go and get your stepladder."

He rushed toward me.

I stepped aside.

He fell into the garden.

He hauled himself up off the ground. "Just you wait. I'm gonna get you."

"I'll let the police know I have a pygmy stalking me.

They'll probably send a pre-schooler over to protect me with safety scissors, so consider this a warning."

"The police," he spat. "You oversized cow, my cousin *is* the police around here."

An awful feeling struck me. "

"Yeah, that's right, my cousin is a cop," he went on. "When I tell him about you, he's gonna lock you up."

Kontos was in front of my building, talking about his cousin, the cop.

"Just out of curiosity, where does this cousin live?"

He grinned.

"Leo's your cousin?"

"Been in trouble with the law already, have you?"

"Look at that time. I have to go." I took off at a brisk clip.

"Yeah, you run, giant," he called out. "Just you wait."

————

I needed a cupcake.

No—I needed cake. Big. Something made to feed twenty. Thick frosting. Sugar accents. Maybe if I asked nicely, Betty would let me pour the batter straight into my mouth, that way it would hit my bloodstream faster.

Betty was waiting, bless her. She slipped a plate into my hand as I walked through the door. "You need this."

A generous slab of marble cake begged me to eat it. All I needed was a ...

Betty held out a fork. "Sit. Eat. Then we'll talk."

I did as she said. Warmth spread through me as I swallowed the first bite and the sugar worked its magic.

Betty beamed. "Good?"

"Better than good," I said with crumb-crusted teeth.

"New recipe. It's a little something my brother is working on."

"Is he here? Because this is a winner."

"He's busy right now. And he's not people person." She patted my hand. "Tell me what's bothering you and I'll see how I can help. Is it the policeman? Because I can mix you up a love potion. My brother can even make a love potion cake. One bite and the detective will be all yours."

"No, I don't think I'm his type."

"If you're sure ..."

A light bulb flipped on in my head. "Before I forget, thank you for the cupcakes. They arrived at exactly the perfect time. How did you get them there so quickly?"

"Messenger."

"Oh." It didn't really answer my real question, but I was getting the distinct feeling there was more to Betty Honeychurch than a bit of mind-reading.

"There's so much more to everyone than what they show us, don't you think?"

I swallowed another forkful of cake. "Do I actually need to speak at all or do you just want to pull it all out of my head for me? Because that would make it easier. This cake is too good to quit."

She smiled sheepishly. "Sorry. You're different to other people, so much more receptive, and I get carried away. Tell me, is your friend still visiting you?"

"As recently as her funeral this morning."

"I'm so sorry. I have a feeling I would have liked Olga Marouli."

I scraped the last crumb off the plate and licked the fork. "Is she going to leave for good. Do you know?"

"Some spirits stay, some move on, and some straddle both worlds forever. I don't know enough to tell you which your friend will be."

That matched what I knew about the dead. Some came and went. I saw them once, twice, a dozen times, then they were gone forever. Others, like the gardener at my apartment building, seemed to be part of a place's fabric. They belonged, and they saw no reason to leave.

"I don't suppose you know who killed her? Could you just reach into the killer's mind and just see? Maybe someone sitting around, thinking about how fun and cool murder is?"

"Some project more easily than others, like you. And others are as silent as the grave."

I blew out a frustrated sigh. "If only it was that easy."

"I can tell you that you need to follow that blonde hair. It will lead you where you want to go."

I'd nearly forgotten the hair. And I had two blondes who struck me as dodgy.

"Three. You forgot about the little man."

She was right.

Jimmy Kontos: little person, jerk, and (maybe most importantly) blond. It wasn't unthinkable that Kyria Olga had opened the door for him, thinking he was one of the local children. And, Leo's cousin or not, he had been hanging around the apartment building and Kyria Olga's knitting group.

My pool of suspects jumped by one extra body. Which meant I had work to do.

"Don't hurry off just yet," Betty said, rising from her seat. "Let me pack you a box."

"You read my mind."

She smiled. "I did."

———

There was no sign of Jimmy Kontos outside my apartment building. That didn't stop me from crouching down and checking behind the shrubs.

Upstairs an email was waiting for me. It was from my old

boss, Sam. I clicked on his mail while I kicked my shoes halfway across the room. I owed him a favor for doing this.

My eyebrows shot upwards.

It wasn't big but it was something. Something *very* interesting.

CHAPTER SEVENTEEN

Angela clutched her chest. "Married?"

"Not any more," I said. "It was brief and a really long time ago. Twenty years."

The shock on Angela's face faded, and a maniacal glint formed in her eyes. "Who was she?" she asked feverishly.

"Does it matter?"

"It matters." She spat the words out like olive pits. "It matters a great deal, because by the time I've finished making that ... that *skatofatsa's* life a living hell, I am going to start on hers. By the time I'm finished she will wish she'd never heard of Pavlos Mavros, let alone married him."

I wanted to point out that the couple were long divorced, but didn't think it would help, especially since they were still so obviously acquainted.

"Oh, in that case, since you're being so rational, I'm happy to tell you who it is," I said.

"I am paying you—remember?"

I'd never seen her like this, eyes blazing, nostrils flaring like a deranged bull. I stepped back.

"Sure, I know you help pay my bills. Consider this a freebie. I'll even toss in some advice, no charge. Get rid of him since you clearly don't trust him. In fact—" I put my hands firmly on my hips and thrust my chin out "—you might give men a miss for a while since the ones you pick always seem to be rotten."

The color drained from her face, and her arm shot out stick-straight, the long pink fingernail pointing toward the door. "Get out of my house or I will make you eat wood!"

I went.

———

Somehow I'd managed to forget all about the reading of Olga's will. I called Stavros Psaris and left a message, apologizing. Kostas, my brother in law, called to let me know my bicycle was ready and waiting for me downstairs. He refused to take my money, which meant I'd have to spoil Patra and Milos rotten.

My email pinged. I dragged myself up off the sofa to check it.

It was from Jimmy Kontos again. This time he was looking for a clothing store for little people in the area. I emailed him a link to an online costume store in Athens with a variety of leprechaun costumes.

He emailed back a cartoon of a donkey's butt.

Another email came through with a serious request. Someone wanted to know where they could get the best cake on the island. I emailed her the address of the Cake Emporium. Betty and her brother's confections were magic.

The phone rang. As usual Angela didn't bother with the pleasantries.

"Pavlos is going out again after work. I just know he's going to see a woman. Could you follow him? Please?"

No apology for earlier, but then I didn't really expect one, not from Angela. "Fine," I said. "But if he's not doing anything suspicious, I want you to promise me you'll drop this."

"Okay, okay," she said, far too breezily for me to believe her.

Soon there would be another man and another request.

———

In my (occasionally) wild and crazy youth I'd been attracted to the smell of sweat and metal. Grease and engine oil would make my clothes slide right off.

Then I grew up.

Nowadays I liked my men reeking of a recent shower and soap.

Clean on the outside, dirty on the inside.

Like Detective Samaras, the little voice inside my head gloated.

I gave the voice a mental kick in the pants and refocused on Pavlos, who was flat on his back, under a blue sedan.

Pavlos and Eleni Kefala. They'd been divorced twenty-something years after just a few months as husband and wife. Who knew? There was a twist I hadn't seen coming. It was funny how the past becomes a repository for all kinds of unwanted baggage.

My butt wiggled on the bicycle seat. My legs were falling asleep and my toes were already tingling with sparkles. I jiggled my feet to try and get some blood flow going. If I caused too much of a commotion, Pavlos would see me.

It was after seven but the air curling through the village smelled like midnight. One by one the lights around town died as Merope's citizens locked up for the night and went home. Kostas had already gone home to my sister, leaving his mechanic to finish up on the sedan.

The light from the garage died suddenly, plunging the area into darkness. Now the only light came from the occasional neon sign and the intermittently-spaced streetlights. Two minutes passed and Pavlos emerged, leather jacket thrown casually over one shoulder. He swaggered down the street. No car. Had Angela confiscated his fancy wheels?

Headlamps painted a wide swath of light on the mechanic.

The car cruised by slowly and stopped alongside Pavlos. He walked to the passenger side and got in. The dome light stayed on for a moment. Enough time and light for me to see them embrace.

Out of the doghouse and into the arms of another woman.

They drove away.

I didn't follow. Didn't need to. The dome light was a silent helper.

I'd recognized Pavlos's companion as Lydia, Kyria Olga's granddaughter.

CHAPTER EIGHTEEN

So Pavlos was previously--albeit briefly--wed to the chilly Eleni Kefala. Then years later, he moved on to the wealthy Angela. And now he was probably in bed with the rebel granddaughter of my dead friend.

The man sure got around Merope, for someone who wasn't a local.

Now where was this all going?

What was I missing here?

In my line of work an pinch of intuition goes a long way. But lucky me, my intuition wasn't intuiting.

———

Another surprise was waiting for me at home.

"You have mail," Kyria Olga said from the chair in front of the television.

I reined my bladder back in and stooped to pick up the slip of folded paper on the floor. "I suppose you read it?"

"No. Did you forget something?" She wiggled her fingers and nodded towards the TV.

Remote in hand, I flicked through channels until Kyria Olga made a happy sound.

"I love this one."

The Notebook. I loved it, too. But tonight wasn't the night.

"Did you see who left the note?"

"Do I look like someone who would snoop?"

"A few days ago I would have said no."

I flipped the note open and smoothed it on my desk.

Tomorrow. The old church at 12:00. Come alone.

Intriguing, but I had no intention of walking into a trap. I slid the paper under my keyboard and decided to sleep on it.

"Kyria Olga, how much do you know about your grand-daughter?" I called out over the weepy movie music.

"Lydia? They call her olive oil because she spreads so easily."

That was helpful. "But how do you know that? Do you know if she's been involved with anyone here in Merope?"

"My doll, she has known half the men in Greece in the biblical way. No doubt many of them were from right here."

That narrowed it down. "You're a big help."

She turned away from the television. "What is your problem?"

"Nothing."

"Well then, *skasmos*! I do not want to miss the kissing scene."

———

Something was pressing down on my chest, restricting my airflow.

My arms flailed.

In the pitch black room, something closed in on my face. I could feel it coming closer. I tried to jump up and ... nothing. I wasn't going anywhere, except my grave.

Something cold and damp touched my face. It rasped up my chin and scraped over my nose with a tiny strip of sandpaper.

My left arm shot out and I flicked on the lamp.

"Get off me, dead kitty!" I huffed.

Dead Cat yawned. Even in the afterlife cats considered themselves superior beings. He blinked and shifted, giving me a chance to roll him off me and onto the bed. He might be a ghost but he had heft. How long had he been dead? And what was he doing hanging around me of all people? Didn't he know I wasn't a cat person?

The beast jumped down to the floor. When I say jumped, I actually mean rolled and plopped. Only there was no noise which freaked me out—as if having a dead pet wasn't weird enough. He hocked up an invisible hairball, and then sauntered toward the door, looking over his shoulder like he wanted me to follow.

I followed. Fat Cat plopped himself down just inside the front door. He looked up at me expectantly. I looked down at and through him. He was sitting on something.

"What have you got there, fella?" I stopped down and waited for him to shift before picking up yet another piece of paper. I unfolded the note. Same hand as the earlier note.

Change of plans. Meet me at four.

What was it Alice had said in Wonderland? Curiouser and curiouser.

This time I laid the slip of paper on the kitchen counter. With the palm of my hand I pressed it flat and stared at it looking for some kind of clue about the author. Dead Cat wound his way though my legs, purring and smooching. I couldn't really feel anything other than a cool breeze against my bare shins. Without thinking I pulled a plastic bowl out of the cupboard and filled it with milk. I placed it in front of the cat and waited for him to drink. Fat Cat stared at me with contempt.

I was pretty sure that meant he liked me.

———

After the cat drama, I couldn't sleep. I tossed and turned for an hour before staggering out to the living room.

When the sun peeped in, I was smiling with satisfaction. It had taken me a month, but I had finally located the missing plate in one of my client's Royal Doulton dining set. It wasn't cheap, but it was within the budget. Another success for Finders Keepers.

The cat reappeared at eight. He sat by the front door, twisting and turning his head as though trying to solve a puzzle.

Seconds later the doorbell chimed. His head twisted around, his luminous green eyes fixed on me as if to say, *I told you so.*

Not wanting to take any chances, I peeped out.

Lydia Marouli.

Why?

I'd never met her and already I didn't like her. Prejudiced? Maybe. But I could smell bad news coming at me from a kilometer away.

I opened the door reluctantly, wishing I had on something snazzier than my pajamas.

"Bare," she said, smokey eyes scanning my apartment.

"Next time I need to redecorate I'll call you."

Her smile was cold. "Funny."

"I try. You've got the wrong place. Your crazy family is across the hall."

She helped herself to my living room, running a long fake fingernail across my desk. "You and my *yiayia* were close."

"We were friends."

"Why?"

"Excuse me?"

"Most people have friends their own age."

"Not once they're out of their teens."

"I get it. Be nice to the old woman whose family is never around, then—*boom*—she goes *kaput*, and you pray she has written you into her will."

"Kyria Olga didn't drop dead. She was murdered." My door was still open. I gave it a little swing back and forth, hoping she'd take the hint. "You can leave now."

"I want to hire you."

Huh. I didn't see that coming. "Why?"

"To find out who killed Yiayia. I know the police are doing their thing, but Merope isn't exactly a hotbed of sin, and the local police haven't had a lot of practice."

Virgin Mary, what was it with this family? They all seemed to despise me yet they were desperate to have me in their business.

"Thanks, but I don't need the work."

The doorbell chimed again. God—who now?

I went the door, expecting Lydia to follow me. She was nearly as annoying as the rest of her family.

It was Leo, and boy-oh-boy did he look good in his jeans, white t-shirt, and motorcycle boots. He looked me up and down appraisingly.

"Hey, where'd you get to yesterday?"

"Around. I couldn't handle the whole burial thing."

"I understand." He stepped past me and froze.

Damn. I'd already forgotten that Lydia was still there. "You have company," he said. He was clearly checking her out.

Lydia ignored him. She was staring down at my counter-top, frowning. Damn, I'd left the second note there.

"Lydia, meet the small-town policeman in charge of your grandmother's murder case. Detective Samaras, this is Lydia, Kyria Olga's granddaughter."

"We've met," he said smoothly.

She looked up from the note and smiled her predatory smile. Damn her perfect hair and nubile figure. "Detective—"

"Samaras."

He didn't invite her to call him by his first name. That gave me hope, although I still hadn't forgotten about his past with my sister.

"Good to see you again." Her long legs covered the room in a flash. Suddenly I felt invisible.

I used my invisibility to sneak across the room and slip the note under my keyboard with the first one. "Oh, you two have met?"

Leo's eyes swiveled my way. "At the cemetery."

"Oh."

"I was just leaving." She batted her lashes at Leo.

"What a coincidence, so was I. We need to talk, if you have time. Coffee?"

"I love coffee," she purred.

"Allie, you want to come with us?" he asked.

"No," I said dryly. "Unlike some people, I actually have a job to do."

Pain flickered across his face. I almost felt bad. Almost.

"See you later?" he said.

"Maybe."

I slammed the door behind them.

"You should not give up on him so easily," Kyria Olga said.

"If you had a neck I'd tie a bell around it. And I'm not giving up on him. To do so would suggest that I was interested in the first place. And I'm not."

She made a tut-tutting sound. "Yes, you are. You will come around and so will he."

"So what, you're a fortune teller now as well as a ghost? Is that some super-secret formerly-living trick?"

""Are you going to that meeting?"

My eyes narrowed. "What meeting?"

"Oh you know, the one in that letter over there?"

"I thought you said you didn't read it."

"That is not what I said." Her eyebrows rose.

"I don't know. I guess so."

"The sooner you figure out who killed me, the sooner they—" she pointed at the wall "—will disappear."

"Don't tease me," I said, padding back to my bedroom. "And yes, I'm going to that meeting. Just as soon as I take care of some other business."

"More important than finding my killer?"

"I have to pay the rent somehow."

———

It takes twenty minutes to ride from my place to the old church. My bicycle knew the way all on its own; I'd been riding this way every week or so for years because my old boss lives close by.

I started nagging Sam the day I finished high school, begging him to take me on as a fetch-it girl. He took pity on me and let me tag along, taking notes and photographs until I proved I was capable of complete discretion and not making a fool of myself.

One day he said, "Guess I could hire you full time. People will tell a skinny white girl things that they just won't tell a gay black man."

He was also my first client when I established Finders Keepers.

Sam was the victim of a hit-and-run that left him in a wheelchair. He hired me to do what the cops wouldn't. It took me a day to find the culprit, a ninety-two-year old woman from the far side of the island, who was too blind to know she'd picked the wrong great-grandchild to drive her to the Super Super Market. The seven-year-old didn't understand the whole stopping to render aid thing, so Sam was going to spend the rest of his life on wheels.

Sam Washington is tall, thin, black, and bald, with a major boner for Luther Vandross.

Oh, and he's an American transplant.

When Luther passed, Sam wept for a week and played Superstar on replay until the neighbors threatened to bounce him into the sea.

Now Sam is my backup. He's my go-to guy when I can't get access to what I need. After the accident signed up for an online college, took every computer course available and spends his days hacking every system on the globe that wants to keep him out.

His skills come in very handy.

"Hey you," I said when the door opened.

"You owe me one, girl." He pulled me down into a big bear hug.

I hugged him tight, then held up the shopping bags. "And look, I bought snacks."

We didn't waste time, tearing into the food like a pair of starving wolves.

"So, Callas, did you get your man?" We sat—me on his kitchen floor, him in his chair, eating fruit salad and rotisserie chicken.

"I thought so, but it's turning out to be more complicated. Somehow Pavlos Mavros is involved with Kyria Olga's death. I can feel it."

"You think he did it?"

"Not really. He doesn't seem to have the motive, but he's tied up with at least one woman who might, but I can't figure out how." I spooned a fat strawberry into my mouth. "Can you run another check for me?"

"Sure, if you've got a name."

"I do."

"It's gonna cost you."

I grinned. "I can pay in advance."

"Steaks?"

"Better than steaks. So much better. As good as it gets."

He gawked at me with disbelief. "No way. Tell me you didn't get your mitts on what I pray you got. "

"Yes way." I wiggled my fingers like a magician and pulled dessert out of the plastic bag. I'd stopped at the Cake Emporium on the way. Betty had the pineapple upside down cake—Sam's all-time favorite—waiting. God, she was *good*.

"If I wasn't old and gay, I'd marry you in a heartbeat. You know how long it's been since I had an honest-to-goodness pineapple upside down cake?"

"Too long?"

"Too damn long. Get the forks."

I watched him dig into the cake before I took my first bite.

"Can I ask you something?"

He swallowed. "Shoot."

"Do you believe in an afterlife? Or is death the end of it —*bang*—game over?"

"Whatsamatter, you dying or something?" He looked genuinely worried.

"No, but I've been thinking about it a lot lately. You know, with Kyria Olga and all that stuff."

"Hmm," he mused. "I thought about it all the time after the accident. You walk around thinking you're immortal, then some old lady and her kid come out of nowhere and change your whole belief system. If this one bad thing can happen to you, then anything bad can happen. You know?"

I had some idea. "So what do you believe now?"

"That our souls go on, but our bodies become dirt."

"What would you do if you saw a ghost?"

"I'll tell you what I wouldn't do. I wouldn't share this cake."

———

I stopped a few meters from the old church. There was no driveway, just a well-worn road of red dirt and fruit trees that, without regular care, had grown wild and twisted. Decades ago, the tectonic plates shifted and rattled Merope's teeth— hard. Greece has earthquakes the way England has rain, but the frequent ground shakers are normally content to rattle picture frames and dinnerware in their cabinets. Not this one. It gave the island a good shakeup and kicked the church in the face as a parting shot to teach us that the Earth, with its swinging moods, was still boss. The rest of Merope recovered, but Ayia Paraksevi was too far gone. The domed roof looked like it had been punched by Zeus. One entire wall was rubble. Mother Nature eventually came in to party, with her weeds. She didn't care about the gold accents or the stained glass windows.

Kids had been coming to the broken bones of Ayia Paraskevi for years to party, far away from the watchful eyes of their parents. How did I know this? I'd been to more than a few parties out here in my misguided youth. It didn't take a genius to know it was still going on; beer bottles with unbleached labels lay scattered around the premises, and a bong made out of a juice container lay inches from my front tire. It, too, was unaffected by the elements. A bunch of someones had partied here as recently as last night.

Some things never changed.

As soon as the big hand hit the four on my watch, I

wheeled my bicycle up to the church. My blind date was late. Or maybe they were waiting inside. Possibly it was a setup. The odds were better than even. Which was why I went in with a can of pepper spray, ready to temporarily blind potential attackers.

The grime-caked windows, with their frames of vine didn't give me much light. Everything was still and quiet. I crept toward the front of the church, where Christ was covered in moss. I took out a tissue and wiped His face off because it seemed like the right thing to do.

"Anyone here?"

My words fell like a rock. No echo. I waited a moment and listened carefully. If anyone was here, they weren't answering.

No people.

No ghosts.

Nothing except a horny cicada, screaming for a mate.

The church was a public urinal for wildlife; the stench of pee, both fresh and stale, hung in the air. The cracked marble shifted beneath my feet, as I crept toward the sacristy.

I sniffed the air again. There was something infecting the church. Something more than urine and stale booze. Something that wasn't a dead rodent in the grip of decay. Too fresh.

A cold fingernail jabbed the base of my spine and dragged its way upwards. Warning signals fired inside my head.

"Hello?" I yelled out again. "I'm armed." Yeah, with non-lethal pepper spray and PMS.

The smell grew stronger. I was getting close now.

Close to what though?

The door handle was long gone, so I pressed on the warped wooden door. It squealed under the pressure.

No dead body as I had feared. Not human anyway. Rabbit.

The air shifted behind me.

I whirled around.

The blow came from nowhere, something wooden flying at my face. I heard rather than felt the wood connect with my skull.

Probably I should have brought police backup. But you know what they say about hindsight.

CHAPTER NINETEEN

When I came to, the cicada was silent. Or maybe I was deaf. I rapped my knuckles on the floor.

Nope, not deaf. Learning sign language could wait another day.

Hand to my head, my fingers searched for the source of the throbbing pain. No blood, that was a good sign. I wiggled all my limbs. Nothing seemed to be broken. More good news. And yet I wasn't exactly feeling the warm fuzzies of personal safety and wellbeing.

With the warped doorjamb to help me, I pushed myself upright.

Black spots.

Spinning head.

Not good.

I fell back onto my knees and retched, but it was all gurgle and no carrots and corn.

Suddenly arms wrapped around me, scooping me up from the filth-crusted floor.

I struggled but the arms held me firm, cradling me. Though it hurt like hell I lifted my head.

It was the guy in black, the one who'd returned my key outside Betty's Cake Emporium. His face was still mostly swathed in shadows, but I'd never forget those eyes. Who was this guy?

"Hey, put me down," I said weakly.

"Not yet."

"Did you hit me?"

"No."

"You're not exactly chatty," I said, and passed out again.

———

When I woke up it was nearly dusk and I was sitting propped up outside the church, around the corner from the front doors. My head hurt and my eyes were gritty.

Shadow Guy was gone.

I found my cell phone and punched Leo's number. It went straight to voicemail, so I left a message.

I was officially one those people who are too stupid to live.

What the hell had possessed me to come out here after receiving a note from God knows who? Anonymous usually meant trouble, especially when it was sending you off to an out of the way place—alone.

Next time I'd be smarter.

Next time? Please—there wasn't going to be a next time. As soon as I got home I was going hand the notes over to the police, tell Kyria Olga I was done, and go on to live my life all alone with my ghost cat and a pile of books. The high points of my day would be drinking coffee and using the bathroom.

I brushed myself off and looked around.

Why had Shadow Guy left me here?

He said he wasn't my attacker, and for some reason I believed him.

What if he'd been attacked next and was dying inside?

To hell with it. With a throbbing skull, I limped back inside, my flashlight app turning my phone into a beacon.

I scanned the battered nave and the shallow transept.

Nothing.

As I closed in on that room behind Christ's back, where the priest used to keep his sacred goodie box, the scent of copper and iron filled the air. The door was still open. I held the bright beam up to pour light into the darkness. Still wobbly, I grabbed the jamb.

Wet.

I yanked my hand away. A streak of blood colored my palm. My insides frosted over. My heart tried hopping away from the rest of me. Somehow I kept it together. What if it was the Shadow Guy and he needed help?

Deep breath. *Don't pass out, Allie.*

I angled my phone and found the source of the blood.

It wasn't Shadow Guy.

It was Pavlos Mavros.

I leaned back against the doorframe while black spots formed in front of my eyes and weaved themselves into a monochromatic kaleidoscope.

"You going to sit on your *kolos* all day or are you going to call the police?"

Pavlos Mavros sat up and climbed out of his body. Another quick comeback; obviously murder was the defining catalyst.

"I'm just getting to that part," I said faintly.

"Unless you killed me, then you had better get busy hiding the evidence."

"Believe me, this is as much a surprise to me as it is to you."

He pulled a cigarette out of his pocket and balanced it on his bottom lip. I guess you really can take it with you.

"I'd help you out, but ..."

"The end is always hazy, I know."

He swiveled around as if looking for something. "Hey, did you see anyone else out here?"

"Just you ... well, your body. Who did you expect?"

He flicked the ash. It dissipated in their air. "Well, time's up, gotta go. Do me favor?"

"If I can."

"Tell Angela I'm sorry. I know she didn't trust me, but I love her and only her."

"I'd love to help, but how am I supposed to slip that bit of news to her? 'By the way, Angela, the ghost of your dead boyfriend spoke to me.' See? Big problem right there."

He grimaced, lips still gripping the cigarette. "You'll figure something out." He thumbed over his shoulder. "You're about to have company. See you on the other side someday."

And on that note, he vanished.

I dialed Leo one more time and left a second message. This time I told him about Pavlos. It would save time to bring the coroner with him.

In the distance I heard the faint wail of police sirens. Something told me they were headed this way, and that they already knew Pavlos was dead.

Classic setup. Duh.

CHAPTER TWENTY

"Silver isn't really my color."

"Sorry, Allie, but we have to take you in." Gus Pappas wasn't laughing. Neither was I. These handcuffs really weren't working for me.

The cops had received a tip that I'd killed Pavlos and was on my way to dump the body, and now here we were.

"Without a car?" I said. "Really? How was that supposed to work? Load the body onto my bicycle and ride him up the hill?"

"He does look heavy," Pappas admitted.

"And I never go to the gym. Ever."

"If it was up to me I'd let you go, but it's not up to me."

"Can we negotiate the cuffs?"

"Negotiating is above my pay grade."

"What *can* you do?"

"Take you in."

'That doesn't really work for me."

He steered me toward the police car. Headlights bumped up the hill.

Incoming.

Leo climbed out of of his black compact. Hooray! The cavalry had arrived. His legs covered the distance in no time.

"What have we got?"

"Sore wrists," I said.

Pappas rolled his eyes. "Callas maybe killed a man. We caught her red-handed, before she could leave the scene of the crime."

I held up my blood-smudged hand. "There was blood on the doorframe. I was trying to steady myself.

Leo had questions. "Steady yourself? Why?"

"I heard a noise so I went to investigate."

"Was this after the attack?"

I nodded.

Pappas's head swiveled from Leo to me and back again. "What's going on?"

Leo filled him in. "Get those cuffs off her," he ordered. "I'm taking her to the doctor."

The cuffs came off and I got into Leo's car.

It was a while before Leo joined me. He took a good long look at what was left of Pavlos Mavros and made some calls. Panos Grekos showed up in his van. He looked happy to not be a solvent courier.

Finally, Leo climbed in to the driver's seat. "You okay?"

"What do you think?"

Then I burst into tears.

He pulled me into his arms. His warm, strong arms. I did my best not to get snot on his shirt.

"You're nice," I said after a few minutes. "It's pity you dated my sister."

"That was a long time ago."

"But it happened."

"We could pretend I didn't."

I smiled through my tears. "Have you met my sister? She'd slit my throat from ear to ear."

Laughing, he pulled out on the road and pointed the car towards the village. "Just for the record, you didn't kill Pavlos Mavros, did you?"

"No."

"Didn't think so. I got in the car the minute I heard your messages. You want to tell me what happened?"

I told him about the notes, the attack, and finding Pavlos's body. I left out the parts where I conversed with the dead Pavlos Mavros and Shadow Guy.

"Did you know him?"

I paused again. "Can I beg some kind of client privilege?"

"You can try, but the courts can compel you to spit it out."

It was worth a shot. "Mavros was the live-in lover of my client, a very wealthy woman. I can't tell you who."

He eyed me sideways. "Why frame you for his murder? It doesn't make sense."

"Who knows?," I said. "Murderers aren't exactly living in the land of sane people."

"Hmm ...." I could almost hear the wheels in his mind turning, grinding up what little information he already had. "So what did you dig up on this guy? Was he hosing this woman for her money."

"He was spending time with his ex wife, and I saw him hugging another woman."

He perked up. "Anyone I know?"

Yeah, your breakfast date.

I couldn't make myself tell him. Not yet. Not without sounding jealous when I had no right to be.

"I don't have a list of all the people you know."

He snorted. "So did you tell your client her boyfriend was fishing elsewhere?"

"No." I thought about my conversation with Angela and her consequent ranting and raging. "But I did tell her he had been married before. She didn't know. It didn't go well."

"You think she could have killed him?"

"Maybe. But she'd never frame me for it."

"What about the other woman?"

Lydia. She was still rattling around in the back of my head as a possible suspect in her grandmother's murder. It wasn't much more of a stretch to think she'd killed Pavlos. But she had no real reason to set me up. We barely knew each other, and hadn't she, this very morning, asked me to investigate her grandmother's murder?

"Doubtful," I said.

Leo bypassed our turn off, taking the road downtown.

"I'm taking you to the emergency room to have that bump looked at. Then I have to take you to the station." He looked at me apologetically, "Just to make a formal statement."

I pressed my head back into the headrest and closed my eyes. "You're just doing your job." My eyes, heavy from injury and stress overload, drifted shut. My mind began its shut-down process.

A finger brushed my cheek. My eyes popped open.

"Hey," Leo said. "You might have a concussion. Stay awake or I'll tickle."

Life was a tough when a woman couldn't even take a nap after a head beating.

One x-ray and several painkillers later, I slumped down into a chair in Leo's office. It was neat and organized with absolutely no personality whatsoever.

"How long have you been on the job?"

"A couple of months. Check it over," he said, swiveling the monitor to face me. "Did I leave anything out?"

"Looks good to me."

"I'm going to need those notes too."

"They're all yours. But I'm warning you now, there's nothing—no name, no envelope."

"Handwritten or typed?"

"Handwritten, looked like a woman's hand. Oh ... fingerprints."

He shrugged. "You never know. Right now it's the only thing we've got besides the body. I realize most of them will be yours." He stood and rotated his shoulders. "Come on, I'll take you home."

"So, I'm not spending the night in the big house?"

Leo grinned. "Not unless you want to. I hear room service is sketchy."

"Home it is then."

I stood, intending flee before Leo changed his mind and decided to dump me in the lockup overnight. But he caught my arm on the way past. He leaned back against the desk pulling me with him, both of my arms in his hands.

"Next time call me when you get the urge to do something stupid." His thumbs brushed over my biceps. Electricity arced through my body.

Wowza.

Alarmed by my reaction, I stepped back and out of reach.

"You don't have to worry about me. I'm a trooper."

"I know, but I can't help worrying."

Just this morning he was schmoozing up to Lydia, and now he was taking the whole love thy neighbor thing to extreme. What was with him?

"Shouldn't you be worrying more about Lydia?"

He grinned, dimples forming in this cheeks. "Jealous?"

I swallowed and tossed my hair back as best I could given my still-aching head. "I don't see anything to be jealous about. I promised Toula I wouldn't touch you."

"You promised her?"

"I had to."

"Why?"

"Because she's my sister and I love her."

He opened the door and held it. "Let's get moving. I have to be somewhere."

As far as days went, this one officially sucked.

Over and out.

———

I woke twelve hours later with throbbing head and a growling stomach. Dead Cat was at my feet, purring loud enough to wake even the really-dead. Satisfied that I was awake, he jumped down and sauntered into the bathroom and waited on the mat while I showered and washed the dirt and blood off my skin.

Afterwards, I was mostly human. By the time I scoffed down two pieces of toast drowning in honey and two cupcakes, I felt up to getting coffee.

I climbed into fresh jeans, pulled on a sweater, and shoved my feet into boots before trying to get a look at my bump in the mirror. I was Damien in *Damien: Omen II,* juggling two mirrors, trying to get good look at the birthmark. Where Damien had three sixes, I had a purple bump. I snapped a picture. Next time someone called me the devil I'd have proof I wasn't.

I dragged myself downstairs, taking the rickety elevator for once, and slouched over to Merope's Best for some liquid wake-me-up. This morning I ordered it extra hot with a second shot of espresso and sucked it down quickly. My eyes hurt too much to read the paper, but from the front page I could tell that the news of Pavlos Mavros's murder wasn't public knowledge yet.

Angela. I had to call her before word spread.

The door of the coffee shop opened and a cluster of people entered. The Marouli clan had arrived.

"Good morning," I said halfheartedly, when they passed

my table. Athena's eyes flicked down to me, but she didn't speak. It was nice to know you could rely on some things to be consistent. No loss really. I didn't want to speak to them anyway.

I sucked down the last of my coffee through the tiny plastic hole and was just about to leave when Tina approached with her pinpricked pupils. Even from a distance the smell of brandy on her breath nearly knocked me down.

"*Gamisou*," she said. "You think you are so important. You are not *skata*. Understand? You are not *skata* on the bottom of my shoe!" She lifted her foot to demonstrate. She toppled backwards.

Without thinking, I reached down to help her up. She slapped my hands away and grabbed the table to pull herself up. She missed and stumbled backwards, crashing into a mug and cookie display. Chocolate chips and tiny bits of ceramic scattered. For a moment I came close to feeling sorry for her.

She made a quick recovery and sank her teeth into my ankle.

"And that, children," I said to the stunned patrons and staff, while I tried to shake her off my leg, "is why you don't drink and do drugs."

"My sister is not a drunk!" George said, coming to her defense at last.

I nodded down at his sister who was crawling around in crumbs and shards. "All evidence to the contrary. Do her a favor and put her in rehab." I glanced over at the counter staff, all in their late teens. "Someone call the police and tell them you have a drunk and disorderly here."

I scurried out of there before I did something silly, like slapping Tina out of her hysteria. Last thing I needed after yesterday was to be on the police radar--*again*--especially now that Leo was pissed at me.

Speaking of Leo, he hadn't said a word on the drive home.

He'd opened the car door for me, for which I thanked him politely, then he followed me up to my apartment and waited, evidence bag open, for the notes. After he sealed them, he was gone.

Not that I was staring or anything, but I did happen to be standing by the window when he came back out of the building half an hour later. He was in fresh clothes and I'd heard the shower going upstairs. Was he going out with Lydia? And if he was going out with her, why was he so touchy-feely with me?

Dead to the world with an egg on my head, I hadn't heard him come home—*if* he came home. I tried not to sulk about it.

Back in my apartment, and buzzing from coffee and Vera's hysterics, I punched Angela's number. I should be doing this in person, but the idea of riding to her place made my heart hurt.

She answered on the second ring.

"I'm so sorry—"

She cut me off. "I cannot believe that stupid *malakas* went and got himself killed."

Of all the reactions I'd expected, that wasn't one of them. "So the police--"

"They came this morning. I told them it was probably one of his *putanas*. Did you manage to find out who he was sleeping with?"

Yes. No. Maybe. "Nothing concrete."

"Too bad," she said, cheerfully. "I would have enjoyed destroying her."

Once I knew Angela was both informed and fine, I settled back down in my office chair and stared at the blank screen.

Two dead bodies. Two common acquaintances. Lydia and Eleni Kefala.

I clicked over to my email.

Incoming.

Perfect timing, too. It was the background check on Lydia, from Sam. And it looked like someone had been a bad, bad girl.

Shoplifting, solicitation, possession of a controlled substance; none of which ultimately resulted in hard time. But it satisfied my curiosity. I turned next to her financials. Good credit. No assets—not unusual for her age— and ... now this was interesting: a deposit of twenty thousand dollars in her savings account the week before Kyria Olga was murdered.

What was that all about? What was Lydia up to? And where had she been when she'd received that payout?

I got up and attacked my closet with a plan in mind. First thing first, find out exactly how long Lydia Marouli had been on the island.

————

You live on a small island long enough and eventually you hear everything about everyone, especially in my line of work.

I'd heard the gossip about Manolis, the owner of the Hotel Hooray. About three years ago his (now) ex-wife paid me to dig deep and drag out all of Manolis's dirty little secrets. I didn't have to look too hard; Manolis had a thing for porn.

Watching porn isn't a red flag, but Manolis had issues. Nobody watches that much porn without risking dehydration and abrasions.

He spent his spare time massaging the mortadella in the hotel office to Huge Natural Racks magazine. One weekend I followed him to the mainland, where he spent ninety minutes watching Backdoor Babes #9 in a grungy theater that reeked of fresh semen and stale cigarettes. Ninety percent of his phone's bookmarks were to porn sites. His computer screen-saver was a winking anus.

His wife left, using her share of the business to finance a lingerie store right here in Merope. Business was booming.

With that in mind, I dug deep in the closet, pulling out a tiny skirt, high heeled sandals and a low cut top. Not blessed with big boobs, I stuffed silicone cutlets into a pushup bra, giving me cleavage that transformed me into Porn Star Barbie's cousin.

Finally, I dipped my face in a bucket of makeup. Even my own mother would have a hard time picking me out of a lineup without her glasses.

Perfect.

I grabbed my purse, rummaged for my keys, then remembered I don't own a car. There was no way I could walk or ride all the way to the Hotel Hooray.

There was only one thing left to do and I really hated to do it.

I called Toula.

CHAPTER TWENTY-ONE

This was going to cost me. Probably a week's worth of babysitting for starters. Could be worse. I could have to spend time with my sister.

Toula crossed herself. A lot. "Do I want to know?"

"New job," I said.

Again with the crossing. "What is wrong with you?"

"Oh, relax. It's a work thing."

"I thought maybe you were acting out after losing your friend."

"Acting out? Toula, I'm not ten. Grieving isn't acting out. And I didn't lose her. This isn't like putting two socks in the dryer and pulling out one. She was murdered. Big difference."

"This is the thanks I get from trying to help you out? Maybe I should just go."

The breath forced its way out of my lungs. "Don't. I do appreciate it. Things are just really weird lately."

"Is this another imaginary friend thing?"

I blinked. "Huh?"

Toula's smile was mirthless. "You don't remember?"

"Would I be asking if I did?"

"Forget it."

"No, no, no. Tell me."

Toula sighed like I was killing her. "When we were kids you had an imaginary friend. A string of them."

Something stirred. Images flashed in my head. Me playing tea party in the backyard with an assortment of dead relatives. My parents looking puzzled when I insisted I wasn't playing alone. People my friends couldn't see. Voices that no one else could hear. I'd forgotten that I used to be so open about my gift.

It all came back. Well, not all. Some. In pieces.

"I remember."

Toula shrugged. "It was weird. Mama and Baba wanted to send you to a psychiatrist."

"I don't remember going to one."

"That's because you snapped out of it pretty much overnight."

"That's because I stopped telling them." I became aware that an underwire was digging into my armpit. I readjusted.

She shook her head. "I'm glad our parents had one sane child."

"Don't be so hard on yourself."

"I mean I'm the sane one."

"You're the family doormat," I said. "How is that sane? Tell me more about this imaginary friend thing. You didn't have them, did you?"

"Forget it."

"Please?"

"Allie, why do you have to be so judgmental? You know my life isn't easy."

"Whose is?" I asked. "No one has a perfect life. And if they say they do, they're lying."

"You do," Toula scoffed. "No husband, no kids, no one

making demands on your time, sucking your soul dry, drop by drop."

"My life is so very perfect. My friend was murdered. My sister is a doormat. And the only sexually attractive guy I've met in years is completely off limits because you used to give him a regular blowjob back in high school."

I'd anticipated ranting and raging, but instead Toula's face relaxed. She pointed up at the ceiling. "Is that where he lives?"

"Yes."

"Have you seen him again?"

"We're neighbors on a small island, and he's working Kyria Olga's murder. Why?"

She shrugged. "No reason."

"We're not seeing each other, Toula. It's purely professional."

Guilt flitted across her face. "I didn't say anything."

"I have respect for your past together. If I dated Leo it would be like some kind of weird incest."

"I don't care. Really." She wiggled her ring hand. "I'm married. With a family. I'm just curious."

I raised an eyebrow.

"Let it go, Allie."

My hand opened; I was done with this conversation. "Keys please?"

She placed the keyring, with its pink T stamped out on a leather apple, in my outstretched palm. "Drive carefully, okay?"

"If anyone rings the doorbell, don't answer. It'll probably be the lunatics across the hall." I filled her in about the episode at Starbucks. Toula was still shaking her head when I left.

Head down, I raced to her car, hoping that no one—especially Leo—would see me. Five minutes later I was pulling in to the parking lot at the Hotel Hooray and sliding out of the borrowed sedan.

The desk was unattended, but the lobby wasn't empty. The former brothel's working girls were hanging out on the couches, fanning themselves.

"You don't want to go in there," one said.

"He's polishing his *poutsa* again," her friend said.

"He spends all day rubbing that thing like a genie's going to pop out and give him three wishes," the first one said.

Her friend mime vomiting. "That doesn't look like a genie to me."

They cackled.

"I'll be sure not to shake his hand then," I said.

Hobbling, I sucked in my stomach, poked out my chest, and walked up to the abandoned front desk. A small bell sat off to the side, so I rang it twice.

There was motion in the back room, and moments later Manolis appeared, zipping his pants, round face sweaty and red. There was no telling what I interrupted and I didn't want to guess. As soon as he realized a woman with thick makeup and few clothes had entered, his frown turned into a leer.

"Well look at you. What can I do you for today?" One hand reached down to adjust his crotch. I thought happy thoughts, like pepper spraying Manolis and kicking him in the family jewels.

"I was hoping you could help me out." I bit my bottom lip and leaned against the counter, pushing my fake assets up higher. If I was lucky they wouldn't pop up and slap me in the eyes.

His unshaved jaw dropped. "You need a bed by the hour or for the night? 'Cause I've got one you can have."

Oh, puke.

"Well, it's like this," I said, batting my eyelashes. "I think a friend of mine is staying with you, and ... I want to surprise her for her birthday."

"What's her name, my doll?"

"Lydia," I said, all seduction and no follow-through.

"I remember her. Very sexy. Very young. Room 104."

"Is she in right now?"

He picked up the phone and dialed. The phone rang out. "No. You want to wait?"

I already knew her room number from the other night. I leaned a little further forward and checked the sign in date. Sunday night. Hmm, which means she wasn't in town, at least not staying here, on the night her grandmother was murdered.

I batted my lashes again. "I don't suppose ... no ...."

"What?" he asked, eyes glued to my chest.

"Well, I sure would like to go in and get a surprise party organized. Maybe blow up a few balloons or something. Maybe bring her a cake."

Manolis folded his arms and chuckled, causing his big belly to undulate. "I want to, but I can't. There are rules."

I bit my lip. "Please?"

He paused. "Maybe I can do something ... if you make it worth my while. You know what I mean?"

Yuck. "What did you have in mind?"

He inclined his head toward the back room. "You could give me a little sugar, in private. Be real good to papa bear."

I did a mental vomit, and thought fast. "I don't have much time right now--and I do like to take my time. Why don't we set a date up for tonight?"

Poor Manolis, dumb as the day was long, bought my lie without question. "Okay, that will work. I close the front desk at nine. Be here."

"Perfect," I purred.

"Let me get the key and I will show you to the room." A

pegboard on the wall held dozens of keys. He plucked one off the hook and shuffled around to where I was standing. He looked me up and down. "You are a tasty little thing. I can't wait to take a bite."

On the inside I was screaming. On the outside I smiled.

I followed him to room 104. He slid the key in, wiggled it, and pushed the door open.

Manolis partially obscured the doorway, ensuring that I'd have to squeeze past him, touching several points on his massive body. I forged ahead, trying to ignore the lecherous smirk on his face. His ex-wife was smart leaving this one behind. But not so smart for having married him in the first place.

I've made plenty of mistakes, but never a Manolis.

Lydia's room was spare with nothing but the basics: queen bed; fiberboard nightstand; cheap lamp with a stained shade; small television mounted to the wall. The closet was a rectangular hole in the wall with a blue curtain serving as a makeshift door. What I presumed was the bathroom was in direct line with the bed. Aside from a half-empty bottle of whiskey sitting on the bedside table, there no apparent sign that anyone was staying here.

"Thanks, Manolis," I said in a baby voice that made me almost vomit in my own mouth. "See you tonight?"

He adjusted his crotch again. "Nine. Be here."

Finally I was rid of Manolis and all alone in Lydia's hotel room. I crossed my fingers, hoping she'd be gone long enough to let me have a good poke around.

I peeked behind the closet curtain first. Women's clothes, all of them tiny and revealing, hung on wire hangers. Blond hairs clung to the black. Definitely Lydia's. Four pairs of shoes, high heels, formed a neat row on the closet floor. This was a woman who loved her shoes. A medium sized suitcase, black hard shell, was pushed to the back.

Taking care not to disturb the shoes, I lifted it out on to the worn carpet. A combination lock sealed the case. I pushed the button. Lucky me, the case popped open. The gods of snooping were smiling in my direction.

A yellow envelope stuffed full of papers was my reward. I slid the contents onto the carpet. Mostly it looked like bank records, and the occasional personal letter. One was signed *Baba*. I wondered if Lydia's father was less chemically dependent than Vera. I hoped so.

Hello, what did we have here?

A birth certificate for a girl born August 15, 1997. My eyes scanned down further. Father: unknown. Mother: Eleni Kefala.

I gasped.

So who was the father? And who was the baby? Was Lydia adopted? Olga had never mentioned a word of it in all the years I'd known her.

The wheeze of car brakes jerked me upright. An engine died just outside the front door. I snapped pictures and shoved the papers back into the suitcase and looked around.

Nowhere to hide.

Wait—the bathroom.

There was one small window above the toilet. If I was lucky I'd fit, but it would be close.

I climbed up on the toilet seat and slid the window open. There's an old adage that if your shoulders will fit through an opening, the rest of you will follow.

Time to find out if it was true.

Peering through the narrow opening, I silently cursed at the ground below. I didn't fancy falling head first onto bare concrete. My head was still had a painful egg that throbbed if I thought about it.

Feet first.

It was the only way.

Thank God I was wearing underwear.

I tossed my torture-shoes out first, and slid my legs through the opening. Through the thin door I heard voices, a woman and a man coming into the room. My Virgin Mary, I should have slid the safety chain home.

"I'll go get us some ice," the woman said.

Lydia.

"Can I use your bathroom?"

Leo.

Uh oh. I wiggled faster.

"Sure."

One thrust and I slid out onto the ground. I picked up my shoes and—

Holy mother of poop from a goat.

My bag was still inside, sitting on the toilet.

CHAPTER TWENTY-TWO

Just when all was lost, footsteps echoed inside the bathroom and stopped. Seconds later, my bag sailed out the window.

I scrambled to pick it up.

"I'm not going to ask what you're doing out there—at least not right now." Leo sounded amused.

Now he was hanging out in Lydia's hotel room? That didn't exactly make me ecstatic.

"Would you believe me if I said I was in the wrong room?" I called out.

"Not a chance."

"Oh." I thought about it for a moment. "You can stand on the toilet and say hello, you know."

I heard shuffling then a loud crack, like plastic snapping. I guess the toilet seat cover wasn't that strong.

"*Gamo tin trela mou gamo*," Leo howled.

In a nutshell: fuck his crazy fuck. Greek loses some of its drama in translation.

"Are you okay?"

"Allie," he said after he ran out of dirty words, "you owe

me, and I'll be coming to collect so you better be prepared to pay up."

I bolted like my butt was on fire.

———

"Hey baby, you wanna come back to my place and check out my velvet art collection?"

I slammed the door of the minivan and spun around. Jimmy Kontos was sitting in his car at the curb outside my apartment building, tying something to his feet.

I squinted. "Are those ... canned tomatoes?"

He rolled his eyes. "Oh, it's you. I mistook you for a woman."

"And I mistook you for a cabbage patch kid. What's with the cans?" Then it struck me. "You're using them to reach the pedals. Why don't you just buy one of those cars with the flipper things or pedal extenders?"

"Because I'm not disabled, I'm just short. You been out standing on a corner again?"

"Yeah, but your mama keeps stealing my customers."

A silver sedan rounded the corner. It was creeping along. Probably the driver was gawking at the hooker and nanos show.

"I hate you."

"I hate you more," I snapped back.

A crack shattered the silence. Wheels peeled, and the smoke and smell of burning rubber billowed in the air.

"*Gamo tin Panayia mou*," Kontos moaned. "I think I'm shot."

"Don't be silly, it was just backfiring."

"So what's this then? Do I look like I'm on my period?"

My gaze traveled down. A blossom of red stained the front of Kontos's jeans, and it was spreading.

"Hurry up and call an ambulance, you stupid giant!"

"Stay with me," I said and dialed.

By the time I hung up sirens were already beginning to howl.

"You're going to have to put your hand on it," Kontos said.

I eyed his crotch dubiously. "Can't you do it yourself?"

"Do you want me to die or not?"

"Is that one of those trick questions?"

"Just put pressure on it."

I pressed my hand against the front of his jeans. "Like that?"

"A little to the left."

I slapped his head. "Don't be dirty."

"Ow. I'm dying here."

I looked down at the wound. It was dark red, not the bright red of arterial blood. No rhythmic spurting. "I hate to say it, but I think you're going to live."

"I'll never get laid again," he moaned.

I raised an eyebrow. "From the looks of it, it's just your leg. Plus when they fix you up you'll have a cool scar to show women."

His eyes closed.

"Don't you die on me!" Mostly I couldn't stand the thought of Jimmy Kontos haunting me for eternity.

The ambulance pulled to the curb. A cop car stopped behind it. The same two paramedics that had detached Maria from Dimitri hopped out.

"You again," one said.

"Hey, Callas, we meet again," Gus Pappas said, grinning. "Trouble follows you around. At least I think it's your face under all that war paint. Maybe we should take you down to booking.

"I was working," I said.

Everyone stopped what they were doing to gawk at me.

"Will you all shut up and get me to the hospital?" Kontos yelled. "Bleeding here!"

The paramedics lifted him onto the stretcher.

Pappas chuckled. "What's the story this time? The dwarf shoot himself to frame you?"

"I'm a little person!" Kontos called out as the paramedics lifted him into the ambulance.

Pappas made a face. "So what's the story, Callas?"

Ten seconds later he knew the full story.

"Did you see the car?"

"It was silver."

"Make?"

"I'm not sure. It looked sporty. If I'd known someone was planning to do a drive-by I would have paid closer attention."

The ambulance pulled away from the curb then stopped. The back doors opened. "Callas? The *nanos* wants you to come along."

"Little person!" Kontos yelled.

Pappas shook his head and pocketed his notepad. "Is he always like this?"

"Pretty much."

"No wonder someone wanted to shoot him."

A dreadful thought struck me. "They did want to shoot *him*, right?"

"What, you think they were after you? Why would someone want to shoot you?"

"Some of my work ..."

"Like Dimitri and Maria? I get the picture. Give me a list and I'll check it out."

"Hurry up," Kontos yelled. "I'm still dying in here."

Pappas nodded. "You go ahead. We'll look for you at the hospital."

I pulled off my heels and ran to the ambulance. The paramedic stood up so I could slide past.

"What took you so long?" Kontas wanted to know.

"The police had some questions." I glanced at the paramedic who had a head start on the paperwork. "You might want to call Detective Samaras, Kontos here is his cousin."

The paramedic blinked, disbelieving. "Kontos?"

"Yeah, that's my name, Jimmy Kontos. You got a problem with that?"

"No," the paramedic ducked his head down and kept writing.

"How come your last name isn't Samaras?" I asked. He didn't look good. If you ignored the wiry beard he looked a whole lot like a sick kid.

"I changed my name."

"You changed it to Jimmy Kontos on purpose?"

"It's my professional name," he said.

The paramedic glanced up. "That's where I've seen you before. You're Jimmy Kontos from *Tiny Men Big Tools*."

"One through sixteen," Kontos said proudly.

Obviously I was still in the dark. "Is that a home renovation show?"

The paramedic's cheeks flushed. "Movies."

"I like movies," I said. "What kind of movies?"

"Porn, you giant mongoose," Kontos said.

I thought about that for a moment. "I didn't realize they made *nanos* porn."

"They make porn of everything," the paramedic said.

Kontos gritted his teeth. "Little. People."

———

"You're still here," Pappas said an hour later.

"You told me to wait," I said.

Plus I felt kind of responsible for the little guy, even if he was a jerk. Jerks need friends too.

"Guess I didn't expect you to follow orders," he said.

I didn't have anything smart to say to that. "Have you caught the shooter yet?"

"We have a suspect."

"Who?"

"I can't tell you. Wouldn't be right."

"There's only half a dozen silver sports cars on the island. Shouldn't take too long to figure out."

"You're no fun."

"I'm lots of fun," I told Pappas.

My phone rang. Toula.

"I have to leave, where are you?"

"It's kind of a long story."

Toula groaned. "Please don't tell me this is something to do with the ambulance I heard earlier."

"Okay," I said. "I won't tell you. You can go head and leave if you like. The van is in the parking lot."

"You've got the keys."

I shut my eyes and cursed.

The hospital doors flew open and Leo rushed in. He leaned on counter at the nurses' station. The leg of his jeans was still wet. Oops. Guess they didn't make toilet lids strong enough to hold six-foot-something of muscled hotness. He ran a hand through his hair while the nurse spoke, then she pointed our way.

I flipped a feeble wave. Leo didn't wave back. He crossed the room in just a few strides.

"You okay?" he asked. His eyes were on me.

"I'm fine."

He nodded. "Okay. Good. Pappas, take her home. Make sure she gets in to her apartment safely. Check every room."

"Why?" Pappas said.

"I'm fine," I said. "I have pepper spray."

Leo gave us a look. "I'll come by later to check on you." His jaw was pulsing with tension.

"Okay, but make sure Kontos knows I didn't leave willingly."

He nodded. "I'll do that."

―――――

Gus Pappas drove me home without incident. He checked over every centimeter of my apartment and stopped to look in my underwear drawer twice.

"Bad guys can hide almost anywhere," he said.

I pushed the drawer shut with my hip. "Trust me, the bad guys have better things to do than hang out in my underwear drawer.

"I have to get out of here," Toula said.

"Thanks for helping me out."

Her smile was tight, but she put her arms around me and gave me one of those motherly hugs. It felt good for a moment. "Call me," she said and left.

It was just me, Gus Pappas, and Ghost Cat, who was using the cop's leg as a scratching post.

"You can leave too," I said to Pappas. "I bet there's a slab of baklava out there with your name on it."

"They can put your name on baklava?"

Oh, boy. "Why don't you go and find out. I'll be fine here."

He looked around one more time, casting a mournful eye at my dresser, and left. I slid the chain home behind him.

Two down. Now it was just me and the cat.

It took seconds to connect the camera to my computer and upload the photos I'd snapped in Lydia's room. It turned out to be a treasure trove of gossipy tidbits. Baby pictures; Tina Marouli and a man I assumed was her ex-husband, holding a baby. Olga's obituary cut from the local newspaper. From the same paper, the front page article about Olga's murder. And the birth certificate.

My eyes scanned the date of birth again. I counted back nine months. The date was smack dab at the end of the time Eleni was married to Pavlos Mavros

I took a quick shower, scrubbed the makeup off and bundled up in yoga pants and an old sweater. Then I grabbed the blanket from the end of the sofa and curled up, the soft woolliness surrounding me. *The Thorn Birds* was on TV. Dead Cat jumped up and began to knead my lap. Satisfied, he curled up and purred. My eyes drooped shut.

"This is my favorite miniseries," Kyria Olga said.

One eye popped open. "Can't I just take a nap? I think I've earned it."

"This is the best part." She gestured at the television. "All that sexual tension."

I sighed and sat up. Dead Cat hissed. I threw the blanket over him and flinched as it wafted straight down through his body. "I was going to yell at you later anyway, so now is as good a time as any to ask you a couple of things."

Kyria Olga sniffed. "I am not a dog you can whistle for when the mood strikes you."

"And yet here you are," I said.

"*Humph*. I do have an afterlife, you know."

"So you abandoned what, exactly, for a 1980s miniseries?"

"Bowling. Genghis Khan was slaying us all. It is no fun when one player has such an advantage."

"I'm sorry I asked."

Commercials flashed on the screen. Kyria Olga turned to face me. "You said you had questions. Well?"

I fold my arms. "Is Lydia adopted?"

Her face went blank for a moment, as though I'd really stumped her. "It has been so long since I thought about it, but yes—yes Lydia is adopted."

"Why didn't you say anything?"

She looked surprised. "Why? It means nothing. She is my granddaughter."

It was a sentiment not often heard in those of her generation, but it added to the affection I felt for my friend.

"I know this is an insensitive question, but I need to ask. Do you know anything of her birth family? Were they local?"

"I am not really comfortable answering that."

"I need to know or I wouldn't ask," I said gently.

Summoning all her melodrama skills, she clutched her chest. "This is not good for my heart."

My brows rose. "You're dead. You don't have a heart, remember?"

She straightened up, making a face. "It was worth a try. Okay. Tina was never a strong person. Even as a child she would cry and cry if Athena took one of her dolls or if George pinched her arm. Neither of my girls were easy to raise. When Tina married, her *baba* and I were relieved that her moods were someone else's problem. By that time we were not even ashamed that we felt that way about our own daughter. George was in the army and Athena was so busy doing her own thing that neither of them was a bother. But Tina, she hung on to us as long as she could." She paused to look at the television longingly. "Her husband wanted a baby. Tina was not happy. She had been a baby, even though she was my our middle child, for so long that she was not prepared to give up the limelight. She was pregnant twice, and she claimed she miscarried both times, but I have always wondered ..."

Crazy Tina in a back room with a coat hanger and a bottle of whiskey wasn't exactly a stretch of the imagination.

"Finally, her husband gave her an ultimatum: baby or divorce. People have a right to choose if they want to have children of course—"

"How very not-Greek of you."

Kyria Olga waved her hand at me. "But before they married Tina had promised her husband she wanted to have children. Who can blame the man for being unhappy when she changed her mind after the vows were exchanged?"

"So they adopted?"

Olga nodded. "There was a young woman in an unfortunate situation wanting to give her newborn child a new family."

"Eleni Kefala," I said.

"Yes," she said, looking surprised. "How did you know?"

"Lucky guess."

She eyed me suspiciously. "Really?"

"No."

She snorted. "Tina made sure that Lydia knew she was adopted from the day they brought her home. Lydia was her baba's little angel of course, but he was working all the time, which left her with Tina."

"So why didn't he take her when they divorced?"

Olga sighed again. "He wanted to take her, and I tried to convince Tina that the best thing for their child was for her to be with her father. But, Tina ... she is selfish. She wanted Lydia because her husband loved Lydia more. That way she hurt her husband *and* won the child. Athena manipulates through bullying, but not Tina. Tina is a snake in the grass. I love my children, but I do not always love their behavior. Tina behaved very badly."

I couldn't disagree.

"I have to go, my girl," she said suddenly. "But we need to talk. And you need to speak with Stavros as soon as possible."

"Why?" I asked, but she was already gone. She'd just told me something important, but with all the mush swirling about my brain, I couldn't figure out what.

The doorbell chimed.

I knew who it was before I even opened the door.

CHAPTER TWENTY-THREE

Leo's face was serious but his eyes were twinkling. "Manolis is looking for you."

I opened the door wide enough for him to come on in. "Let him look."

"I suppose you have a good reason for hiding in Lydia's hotel room?"

"Would you like a drink?" My tone was sticky sweet.

"Sure, that'd be great."

"Too bad. I hear other policemen down in hell are waiting for beer."

"We're Greek Orthodox. We don't believe in hell."

"True."

He exhaled and flopped down on the sofa. "What do you want?"

"What do I want? Nothing. You're the one who knocked on my door, remember?"

"You want to get something to eat?"

My eyes narrowed to tiny slits of suspicion. "Like a date?"

"If you like."

"I bet Lydia would like to go out for dinner."

"Would you like me to call her?"

I felt a plan coming on. Hopefully the ghosts would stay away. "No. Tell you what, let's order a pizza, my treat."

His smile turned into a grin. "Okay, that works for me. Vegetarian?"

I snorted. "Meat, cheese, and a big thick crust."

"It's like you know me."

I phoned in the order. "How is your cousin?"

"He's going to live. No major damage."

"That's great."

"He was annoyed that you left. He said to tell you he expected nothing less from a giant."

I rolled my eyes. "Ungrateful creature."

"I think he likes you," he said.

Could have fooled me.

The pizza arrived in the hands of a pimply teenager twenty minutes later.

"Is that a roach leg?" I pointed at something stuck on the cheese.

Leo prodded at the offending object with a finger. "Nope, I think it's a ... rubber band. From braces. You want me to take it back?"

"Hell no," I said, plucking the hot rubber from the topping. "I'm too hungry to care."

Like a pair of starving wolves we bit into steaming slices, hot cheese sticking to our chins.

After we emptied the box, we slumped on opposite ends of the couch.

Leo flicked through the television channels finally settling on the evening news. It was a slow news night, and once again the anchors were discussing sports scores and an incoming storm.

"Is that going to affect your crime scene at the old church?" I asked.

"No, we're done out there."

"Do you have a match on the handwriting from the notes?"

"Not yet. We checked against the victim. It wasn't a match."

"So ... any leads?"

"None that I can share."

Damn his professional integrity. I was getting absolutely nothing from him. So much for buttering him up with hot, fresh pizza. If he was immune to that, he'd be immune to nearly anything.

I should have ordered beer.

"Didn't get much out of me, did you?" Leo asked.

I blinked. "Who, me? Would I buy you dinner in order to pump you for information? Do I look like I'd do something like that?" I stood and stretched, trying to relieved the pressure in my stomach. I waddled into the kitchen to get water.

Dead Cat was curled up on the countertop, the tip of his tail flicking. He began to purr as I reached past him. I hated to admit it, but I was really starting to enjoy having him around.

Leo followed me into the kitchen. He was oblivious to the giant cat. "So when are you going to tell me what you were doing in Lydia's motel room?

"See, it's like this," I said. "I wasn't planning to."

"But it's okay to try and get me to talk about my case?"

"All is fair in love and information seeking."

"What were you looking for?"

Dead Cat glared at Leo.

"Her beauty secrets. I, too, want to learn how to dress like I belong on a street corner. Are you satisfied?"

"You looked like you were doing a pretty good job this afternoon."

"Ha!"

He grabbed me by the shoulders. In one move he pushed me up against the wall. "Am I going to have to get physical with you?"

"Go on, big boy, I dare you. That'll look good on your record. Doesn't the department frown on slapping women around?"

"I'd never hit a woman," he said, sliding his knee between my legs and pressing forward. A small gasp slipped out of my lips.

"So what did you have in mind?"

"I'm planning on fucking all your secrets out of you."

"Mmm," I said. "That will never happen."

"Don't be so sure." His fingers tangled in my hair. "I'm very persuasive ... and very, very good."

"I don't want to be another notch on your holster."

His laugh was husky in my ear. Lips skimmed my earlobe. A river of lightning zoomed down to my girly bits, causing an instant bonfire.

"There aren't that many notches." He spoke so softly that I could barely hear him. Goosebumps popped up all over my neck, despite the warm breath from his mouth. Hand still entangled in my hair, he tugged gently until my head tilted, revealing my bare neck.

God help me, he smelled good. He had that clean freshly showered smell of soap and man. The same leg that had separated my thighs was slowly rubbing against my groin. The flames inside me licked higher. In that moment I was desperate to have Leo inside me.

"Did you do this with Lydia?"

He pulled away from my neck and looked into my eyes. "No," he said, simply. Right then I believed him. Then his mouth covered mine.

I broke away again. "I promised Toula I wouldn't touch you."

"You're not touching me. I'm touching you."

He had a point—besides the one between his legs that was pressing right up against me.

My house phone rang.

"Leave it," Leo growled.

It rang six times and then I heard myself spitting out my wooden message. A moment later Toula's voice filled the kitchen.

"*Panayia mou*, Allie? You didn't tell me that ambulance was there for a shooting. Why didn't you say something? Hello? Pick up if you're there." There was a pause, then, "Also, could you not tell Leo I asked about him. Call me back."

Well, that was that.

I slid down the wall and wiggled out from under Leo. Toula was a bucket of ice on my libido.

"I can't do this," I said.

Leo exhaled and rubbed the back of his neck. "You sure?"

No. "Yes."

"Okay. I understand."

"Sorry about the blue balls," I said.

"Don't sweat it." One side of his mouth lifted in a sexy half-smile. "I know you still want me."

"I never said I didn't. It's just not the best idea in the world."

A phone rang again. This time it was Leo's cell. He glanced at the screen and sighed. "I've got to go."

"Go," I said lightly.

He took my hand and pulled me to him. He lifted my chin with a finger and pressed a gentle kiss on my lips. "We're not done yet. We haven't even started."

I wanted to believe him.

———

The rest of the night passed without anyone else trying to get in my pants or kill me. Waking up in the morning is always a good thing.

The sun was hiding this morning, and there was little traffic. I showered, dressed, and jogged across the street for coffee. I was coming out, coffee in hand, when a car approached.

My muscles tensed.

Champagne colored paint. Tinted glass. It slowed and cruised alongside me.

Crack!

This time I wasn't taking any chances. I hit the ground and rolled toward the coffeeshop, waiting for pain and blood.

"*Re*, what are you doing?"

I lifted my head. The driver was a kid who looked too young to have hair around it. I couldn't remember his name but I knew his face. He was almost half my age.

"Did you just shoot me?"

He looked confused. "Why would I shoot you?"

I sat up and checked for bullet holes, just in case. "I don't know. Why did you slow down?"

He grinned. "You want to have sex?"

Greek guys are so forward they're backward. Greece is the butt-pinching capital of the planet.

"Ugh. No!"

"How about a little *tsibouki*?"

"No!"

"You could use your hand."

"Are you kidding me? I know your parents!" I pulled out my phone and pretended like I was going to call them.

"*Gamo ton kerato mou*," he said and sped away.

I sprinted home, relaxing when the chain slid home. Was it going to be like this every time a car backfired? How was I supposed to ride my bicycle from A to B without flipping out?

An idea popped into my head.

I jogged upstairs and knocked on Leo's door.

He was already up and dressed and--I inhaled deeply--he smelled like soap. I tried not to melt on the floor.

He grinned. "Want to come in?"

"Yes, but also no. I need a favor."

"You didn't come here to finish what we started?"

"No."

He leaned against the jam. "What then?"

"I need to borrow your cousin's car."

"No."

"It's not like he needs it, and you still haven't locked up the shooter. What if they come back for me? What if they wanted to shoot me in the first place? I can't ride my bike everywhere. Besides, he'll probably appreciate someone driving it around so the tires don't get all wonky."

"What are the chances you'll drop it if I say no."

I squinted. "Zero."

"If he finds out you're driving it, I'll tell him you stole it."

"Deal."

He gave me the keys. I was mobile again.

Now that I knew that Eleni Kefala was Lydia's birth mother and Pavlos was the father, it was time to talk to Eleni. I was on the verge of cracking this all open, I could feel it.

I had two blondes and two dead bodies. I'd scratched Jimmy Kontos off the suspect list already, given that he was in a hospital bed with a bullet wound. He wasn't tall enough to strangle Kyria Olga or bash Pavlos Mavros' skull in. Not without a ladder, anyway.

Next I stopped at the More Super Market for a bottle of aspirin and toilet paper.

"Someone is mad at you," Stephanie Dolas said when it was my turn at the checkout.

"Who?"

"Maria. She had her lips done and it went badly."

I rolled my eyes.

"I wouldn't mess with her too much," Stephanie said. "Look what happened to Kyrios Moustakas."

"That was an accident." I gave her a ten euro note.

"It looked that way."

I raised an inquiring eyebrow at her.

Stephanie gave a small one-shouldered shrug. "Kyrios Moustakas saw Maria kissing Kyrios Vlahos, and he told Kyria Vlaho. And look what happened." She drew a finger across her throat.

I winced.

"Maria knows Kyria Vlaho hired you to get proof. I would be careful if I were you."

I picked up my change and snatched the sack off the counter. So Maria was probably a murderer. Whatever happened to the good old days when teenagers just smashed each others kneecaps?

I dialed the police station again. Pappas answered.

"Merope Police Department."

"It's Allie Callas. I think I just did your job for you."

"Are you wearing those cute little panties with the flowers?"

I rolled my eyes. "Which ones?"

"The purple ones."

"No. Now concentrate, Pappas. Maria Stamatou killed Vasili Moustakas, and I bet she drives a silver car now."

"Maybe she does, maybe she doesn't," he said cryptically.

I ended the call. It was time to talk to Eleni Kefala.

CHAPTER TWENTY-FOUR

Eleni Kefala's home was one of those perfect cottages you see stamped on postcards and in glossy picture books about Greek islands. White. Two story. brilliant blue shutters. Dozens of beautiful flowers whose names I would never know reached out toward the sun in an organized, elegant jumble in her yard. She even had a view of the sea.

I spotted Kyria Eleni kneeling amongst the flowerbeds, digging with a claw tool, a raffia hat concealing most of her smooth blonde hair.

She stood as I approached, taking care to slip off her gardening gloves and set them aside. Her face was a neutral mask of cool politeness.

"Can I help you?" she asked.

How much to say? I battled that question all the time in my line of work. Sometimes less was more; and sometimes more was, well, more successful. I suspected that underneath her smooth veneer Kyria Eleni was harder than the Hope Diamond, and that if I wanted anything out of her I was going to have to be serve up honestly ... with just a twist of deception.

I introduced myself as Kyria Olga's friend and neighbor, and mentioned that I was investigating her murder. The ice queen didn't flinch.

"Yes," she said. "Kyria Olga and my mother were friends. I do hope the police find her killer soon; none of us are safe until then."

"I don't know about that," I said, looking at the flowers.

One perfect brow arched upwards. "Oh?"

"Both the police and I think it was personal. So, chances are there's not a psycho serial killer buzzing around town looking to strangle another old lady."

"Really." Her voice was dry and cool.

"Anyway, I don't suppose you know Olga's granddaughter, Lydia?"

"She has grandchildren? I'm not all that familiar with her family tree."

"Surprising," I said, "since you and the Maroulis kids all grew up together right here in town."

The side of her mouth twitched again. "Where, exactly, are you going with this? I have things to do."

"Well, it's like this." I handed her a photograph of the birth certificate I'd found in Lydia's case. The healthy glow of her cheeks faded a touch.

"What do you want? Money?"

"No. And I won't be sharing this with anyone else." My voice softened. "I just want some information, that's all. Your secret is safe."

She looked around, as if checking to see if we were being watched. "I am probably going to regret this, but let's talk about this inside."

I followed her into the house. In soft colors and with tasteful, serene art, her decorating skills were worthy of a magazine layout.

"You have a beautiful home." I meant it.

"I hope you don't mind if I don't offer you a drink." She led me to a sunny parlor at the back of the house. Floor to ceiling windows revealed a back garden as beautiful as the one in front.

"I won't take it personally."

"You should. Please, sit."

"Does your mother live with you?"

"No. She lives in a home that can take better care of her needs. Her mind isn't what it used to be."

"I'm sorry. That can't be easy for you."

"Why are you sorry?" She threw one slim leg over the other and leaned back in her chair. "So, what do want to know? How I ended up pregnant with a child I didn't want and gave it away?"

"I'm sure you did what was best."

"I did what was best for me."

"Kyria Eleni, is Lydia your daughter?"

"No, but I did give birth to her—or so she claims."

"She confronted you?"

"She tried. I told her to leave. It was a long time ago. I have no connection to her now."

Eleni Kefala was the coldest fish I'd ever met. I actually felt sorry for Lydia

"How did she take it?"

"She demanded to know who her father was. I told her it was none of her business."

"So who was her father?"

"Who cares?"

I shrugged. "Did you hear about Pavlos Mavros's murder?"

If looks could kill, I'd be confetti. "Sad, but that is none of my business."

"You were married."

"It's not a secret."

Except to the citizens of Merope. "So why don't you tell me why Lydia came looking for you. Why now?"

"I don't know. Ask her." Her face relaxed back into a blank mask. "No more questions. Mind your own business or you might find yourself in some serious trouble."

"That almost sounds like a threat."

"I want to be left alone, and I want the past to stay right where I left it."

Eleni Kefala had something to hide, and like a dog with a tasty bone, I was determined to dig right to the core to find out what that something was.

Even if it did bite back.

————

I napped. Because that's what people in Greece do on a warm day—even a warm autumn day. While I was sleeping, the players and pieces tap danced around my head. And then suddenly—*click*—I could see what might have happened to Olga and Pavlos. I needed to see the crime scene photos, which meant I needed Leo's help.

I jumped out of the bed, pulled on the pair of jeans lying on the floor and a Billy Idol concert t-shirt circa 1985 that I'd scored in a thrift shop on the mainland. There was no time to waste with phone calls; I bolted upstairs to Leo's apartment and pounded on the door.

Lydia opened the door. "Oh," she said, "it's you."

A scream bubbled in my chest. This wasn't the time for a jealousy-fueled hissy fit.

"I need to speak to Leo."

She flipped her blonde hair back off her shoulders. "Fine. I'll tell him you're here." Before I could say anything she shut the door in my face.

Moments later the door opened. Leo was there in the

same clothes he'd been wearing earlier. "Hey," he said softly and leaned in to kiss me on the lips.

I pulled away, shooting death rays at him. "This is business, not pleasure. I need to see the crime scene photos from Olga Marouli's murder."

"Why?"

I took a deep breath, trying not to let tears bubble up in my eyes. "Look, if you're not going to help—"

"Let me grab my keys and we'll go.

"Please tell me your girlfriend isn't coming along with us," I said archly.

"Who? Lydia?" He had the nerve to look all surprised and innocent. "Look, she just showed up. I didn't invite her."

"Save it," I said, turning to go back down the hall. "It's none of my business. I'll meet you downstairs."

By the time Leo hit the bottom of the stairs, I'd regained my composure and steeled myself for the worst. Lydia was just behind him, and was it my imagination or was she pouting a little?

"You ready?" Leo asked, looking like he actually cared.

I nodded and climbed into his car. He and Lydia exchanged a few words I couldn't catch, then he joined me.

"You want tell me what this is all about?" he said.

"If I'm right."

"Okay, that's really all you're going to say for now?"

"I don't want to be premature."

He shook his head and laughed. "Whatever it is you're thinking about Lydia, you're wrong."

————

Glossy photos covered Leo's desk. Each of them contained a different angle, a different close up of my dead friend. Elbows on the table, I inspected each one and tried to disassociate.

"Want coffee?" Leo offered.

Still focused on the pictures, I nodded. "can I have the ones from the Mavros murder as well?"

Leo paused. "Are you sure you want to see them? They're gruesome."

I looked up at him. "I found him, too, or did you forget?"

"Right," he said shortly, and left me alone.

Suddenly Dead Cat appeared. I jumped back, surprised to see him here of all places. It seemed he was attracted to me, not just my apartment. The fat marmalade cat strolled back and forward over the photographs, leaving no evidence of his travels. Finally he stopped and began to knead, his jellybean toes flexing and contracting. Old habits die hard.

He stopped kneading and fixed both green eyes on me. I felt like he was sending me a message.

"What is it?" I gave a little wave and he backed up, revealing the photo beneath his dead butt.

The photo was a closeup of Kyria Olga's face and neck. Black-blue bruises. Chalky soft skin. And there on her cheek was the tiny smudge of dirt I'd noticed before. Dirt or something else?

Dead Cat meowed and jumped through a wall.

Leo returned with coffee. A file was tucked under his arm.

"Check this out." I slid the picture over to him. "I don't suppose the lab analyzed the smudge on her cheek?"

"We and had to send that sample to the mainland. Should be back at the end of the week. Why?"

"Just wondering," I said, shrugging. "Is that for me?" I nodded at the folder in his hand.

"Don't say I didn't warn you."

I ignored his warning and flipped the folder open. Up close and personal, the sight of Pavlos Mavros's body was horrific. The back of his skull had caved in like a rotten melon.

My gag reflex gave me a poke, to remind me it could make things messy for me at any time.

Photos spread out in front of me, I pored over them, looking for something I didn't yet understand.

Then I saw it.

That one tell.

The smear on her cheek. The dirt.

———

"You want to what?" Leo said as he pulled up outside our apartment building.

"It'll just be for an hour or so. My driving record is clean."

"I know," he said. "But still ..."

"Fine. I'll walk or ride my bike."

"I'll take you. Just point the way."

"It's a persona mission," I said, starting to feel pissy. "It's the least you can do."

"For what?"

"For being Toula's ex-boyfriend."

Leo sighed. "I'm not going to win this, am I?"

"Nope." I held out my hand. "So you may as well just hand over the keys."

He climbed out of the car, leaving the keys in the ignition.

"I'll be back," I told him.

He stood and watched until I could no longer see him.

———

The young fresh faced woman in the open doorway bore no resemblance to the Lydia I'd met so far. Scrubbed clean of the heavy makeup and dressed in trendy sweats, she looked all of sixteen years old.

Like jailbait.

Lydia stood in the open doorway of her motel room, tapping one foot and staring at me as though I was a cockroach. Or a rival. Same thing, really in woman-speak.

"I was wondering when you'd show up," she said.

I was surprised. "You were?"

"Sure. I saw you at mommy dearest's place, then when the creep at the front desk asked where my friend was, I knew you'd been here. Did you find what you were looking for?"

"I wasn't looking for anything in particular. It was more of a shake-the-tree-and-see-what-happens kind of thing."

"And you found my birth certificate--the real one."

"I did. And I have questions."

"Of course you do," she said. "You want to know who my birth father is."

Once again I was surprised at how sharp she was. "Actually," I said slowly. "I think I know. Pavlos Mavros. He was your father wasn't he?"

"Yeah."

"How did you find out?" I asked gently.

She met my eyes. "Actually, he found me. About a month ago. I didn't believe him at first but then he had pictures of him and her back in the nineties."

"Why did it take all these years for him to find you?"

"The bitch threw it in his face that he had a daughter and she'd given me away. They were only married for brief time-- but you already know that."

"I did, but why now? Why use it against him now?"

Her look said, you're kidding, right? "Because he wanted to get married again, to that rich lady. And it really pissed Eleni off."

"She still considered him her property."

"I liked him, you know, although I already have a father. It would have been nice to get to know him better ... as sort of a friend, you know?"

"That's understandable. There's no rule that says he couldn't be part of your life too."

"Right. I wouldn't have loved Baba any less. But now ..."

"I know this is a sensitive question but you're smart, so I'll ask it directly. Who do you think killed Pavlos?"

"Her, of course. Don't you? *Gamo*," she said, snapping the band in her hair. "It's been the week from hell."

I closed my eyes and sighed. "You've got that right." I remembered the huge deposit in her account. "What about the money, the twenty thousand?"

"Eleni gave it to me to go away."

"Cold," I said.

"I'm hoping to fight genetics." Lydia smiled coolly. "There's something I have to know before you go."

"Shoot. Unless it has to do with Detective Samaras."

"No," she said. "It was a first, but I made a complete idiot of myself there. He's all yours. Unless of course you don't want him."

Her words perked me up. "He's my sister's ex. That doesn't mean I don't want him. It just means I can't touch."

She made a face. "Ugh."

We both nodded together. It was a sucky situation.

"So what's your question?" I was eager to get out of there now.

"Manolis. What did you promise him to get him to let you in here?"

A touch of the devil entered my grin. "I promised him you'd go on a date with him," I lied.

Lydia's grin matched my own. "You're evil. I like that in a person."

As I drove away in Leo's car I decided I actually sort of liked her. And not just because her smart mouth reminded me, well, of me.

———

"Now you are getting somewhere," Kyria Olga said from Leo's passenger seat.

I swerved slightly then righted the steering wheel. "Could you not do that while I'm driving?"

"You would think a woman close to the truth would be happier," she sniffed. "Especially if she had been doing kissy-kissing with a certain policeman."

Clearly nothing was sacred. "Can't anything stay private?"

"No. The Previously Living love to watch over the living. You are like a soap opera."

The idea of all my dead relatives watching way back when I lost my virginity was decidedly revolting and unsettling.

"So you're a voyeur?"

"I would love to see you settled down with a good man."

"And if I want to be alone?"

"I am Greek and I am old—"

"You mean dead."

"—so I believe it is better to be miserable with someone than happy alone. Your parents need grandchildren."

"They have grandchildren."

"Grandchildren are gold. No Greek grandparent can ever have enough grandchildren. Now where are we going?"

"To see Eleni Kefala again. She and I have unfinished business."

"I was afraid of that."

"Don't worry, I'm armed," I said, patting the pepper spray in my purse. But there was no reply, she was already gone.

———

Other than the porch lights, all was dark at Eleni Kefala's cottage home. I looked at my watch, 8:28 P.M. Not exactly the witching hour. She was probably watching television with the lights off; I do the same thing.

I hammered on her doorbell twice and waited. A noise penetrated the darkness. A kitten mewling? Or something else?

Holding my breath, I listened. There it was again. Inside the house.

The front door was locked tight, so I ducked around the back to the twin French doors with dotted Swiss sheers. Something was inside, on the floor.

Someone.

Someone that looked like Eleni Kefala.

Virgin Mary, I hated to have to do this but I had no choice. Let her bill me if it came down to that. I picked up a potted gardenia and hurled it at the glass. It cracked and fell, making music as it landed. I flipped the lock, and finally the handle turned, allowing me to open the door.

Eleni reached for me. "Help."

But I couldn't. I was already falling to the ground beside her.

CHAPTER TWENTY-FIVE

Leo arrived at the same time as the ambulance. He didn't look happy.

"What are you doing?" he asked, checking me out to answer his own question.

"I don't know. I rubbed the back of my head. My egg was now twins. "I might live."

He shook his head. "Worrying about you is going to send me to my grave."

"You're worried about me?"

Leo pulled me to him and stamped a kiss on my hair. Then he steered me toward the ambulance.

"Stay right there," he said, then to the paramedic, "Patch her up. If she tries to move, sedate her."

"Hey, that's not fair!"

"I can't do my job if you're running around. Stay."

The paramedic checked out my bump. "Good news, the skin's not broken. Have you got a headache?"

"I just got hit on the head, what do you think?"

She stuck a cold pack on the bump. "Nausea?"

I shook my head.

"Any loss of consciousness?"

"Not since I woke up after being whacked in the head."

By the time I answered all her questions, Leo was striding back up the path.

"Do I want to know what you were doing out here?"

I winced. "Trying to convince her to join my cult?"

He folded his arms. "Try again."

"I was sticking my nose in where it doesn't belong?"

"Sounds mostly true. What else?"

I promised Kyria Eleni I wouldn't reveal her secret, but that was before someone hit me over the head in her house.

"Eleni Kefala is Lydia's birth mother."

He blinked "She's what?"

I exhaled, resigned to telling him more. "Lydia's birth mother. Pavlos Mavros was her father."

He folded his arms and waited.

"Eleni and Pavlos were married for a while back in the nineties. After they separated, Eleni found out she was pregnant and adopted the baby--Lydia--out to Tina Marouli. Fast forward to a couple of weeks ago, and Eleni flipped out when Pavlos told her he was planning on proposing to Angela. She came clean and told him about the child she'd given her away. So Pavlos tracked down Lydia. And here we are."

His face was stoic. "How do you know all this?"

I shrugged. "I asked the right questions?"

"And you think Eleni Kefala killed Pavlos?"

"Probably."

He looked surprised. "Motive?"

"Grudge. Revenge. I'm not totally sure. But she wasn't glad that Pavlos found Lydia, or that he wanted to marry someone else."

He studied me for a moment longer. "Anything else?"

I shook my head, holding the cold pack with one hand.

"Good. I'm taking you home."

"But Eleni--"

"She's unconscious." Wheels clacked, and the paramedics rolled the stretcher up to the ambulance doors.

I moved aside and took a long look at Eleni. She didn't look good.

"You probably saved her life," said Leo. He took my arm and lead me to his car.

"Question," I said. "If Eleni is unconscious and I was attacked, who hit us?"

"I don't know."

I stopped. "Wait, I have to go back in."

"It's a crime scene."

"It's important," I said, and jerked my arm free. The cold pack fell.

I found what I was looking for by the phone: a small address book, dotted with flowers. I pocketed the book and ran back to where Leo was pacing.

"Take this." I pressed the book into his hand. "You'll find the handwriting matches the notes I gave you."

––––––––

The next morning I was on the couch, fiddling with my double eggs, staring at the ceiling. No one bugged me—alive or dead.

Eleni Kefala. Had she really killed Pavlos? And what about Kyria Olga? How did Eleni fit into that equation? It might make sense if Eleni had showed up at Kyria Olga's apartment, hoping to use a grandmother's love to pressure Lydia into staying away. Kyria Olga wouldn't have stood for that.

Boom. Argument. Eleni Kefala loses control.

But now with the attack on Eleni, my theory was soggy.

I was out of plausible theories. Everything else was just ridiculous.

As soon as the clock struck a decent hour, I hobbled upstairs. No Leo.

I slogged across the street to get coffee. *Frappe*. Cold and foamy. I needed at least two.

The Maroulis clan were all piled into Merope's Best. I kept my head down and ordered my coffee, determined to stay out of their way. Last thing I wanted was to be on the end of another of Tina's outbursts.

I couldn't help glancing over at their table on my way out. Both boys flipped a one-fingered greeting. I ignored them.

Outside, Dimitri Vlahos was crossing the street. He turned tomato-red when he spotted me.

"Don't you say a word," he said as he neared.

"I wasn't going to."

"*Skeela.*"

An engine roared, and suddenly three-thousand pounds of metal came hurtling toward us.

Kyrios Dimitri froze beside me.

I grabbed his hand and pulled.

The car zoomed by like a silver streak.

Kyrios Dimitri didn't have time to yell. His body hit the hood and bounced. Blood splattered. Tires screeched as the driver hit the breaks. The car spun, once, twice, and a third that ended prematurely when it hit a pole.

At first I thought the driver was dead too, but Maria got out, dressed in a schoolgirl outfit. Something was seriously wrong with her mouth. Lip filler gone rogue.

"Why won't you die?" she screamed through those horrifying lips.

I looked down at what was left of Dimitri Vlahos. Burning bile flooded my throat.

"Um ... I think he's dead," I said.

Maria staggered toward me. "Not him—you." She dropped to her knees and cradled Dimitri's head in her lap.

Behind me, someone started to scream.

That's when I realized there was something in my hand. I looked down and saw Dimitri's arm, my hand still holding his.

———

"I'm not saying anything," Pappas said when he arrived. "Just go to the station and help yourself to the forms. You know where we keep them. Oh, and fix yourself a cup of coffee too. Maybe put your feet up on the table."

I went.

Is Detective Samaras around?" I asked the receptionist.

"He's in his office."

"Thanks." I started down the hall.

Leo was at his desk, shirtsleeves pushed up, scribbling on a stack of papers. He didn't look happy.

"Hey," I said. "Can I come in?"

His mouth eased into a smile, but his eyes remained clouded. "Hey yourself. How are you feeling?"

"I'm thinking about running a marathon."

I held out my hand. It was shaking.

"What's going on?" Leo helped me to a chair and crouched down. He took both of my hands in his. "Is that blood?"

I looked down. Bits of Dimitri Vlahos were on my shirt. "It's nothing," I said.

Leo's phone rang. He flipped it open and listened. "Yeah, she's here," he said after a moment. He kept his eyes on me the whole time. I didn't like where this was going.

He clicked the phone shut and exhaled. "They're bringing

Maria in. Apparently she admitted to shooting Jimmy. The bullet was meant for you."

"Will she go to prison?"

"She killed a man."

She wouldn't have much use for her new nose in prison.

"I should probably go," I said and stood on shaky legs.

"You want me to take you home?"

"I'll be fine. I have some errands to run."

"Like what?" His eyes narrowed.

"I might go by the hospital and visit your cousin."

He looked unconvinced. "He'll like that. He placed one hand on each cheek and kissed me. It might have been soft but there was real heat just behind that kiss. And tongue.

I still felt shaky, but now it had more to do with that kiss than murder.

————

Jimmy Kontos was living the high life in hospital. Sure he was bandaged up and confined to a hospital bed, but he had constant television, snacks, and twenty-four hour nurse care. What's not to love about that?

Apparently everything. Something whizzed by me before I even stepped in the room. I picked the offending object up off the floor. Chocolate. Yum. And it was wrapped in foil, so no need for the five-second rule.

"It's all your fault that I'm trapped in here," he said and hurled another chocolate. This time I caught it. Now I had two. If he kept this up I'd have a whole box.

"That's right, it's all my fault some crazy teenager shot you."

He perked. "A teenager huh? Is she hot?"

"If you don't mind plastic. Probably not going to look so hot in those prison uniforms though."

"Nobody's perfect." His face fell, then brightened. "Maybe I should send some of my videos to cheer her up."

I unwrapped one of the chocolates and popped it in my mouth.

"Hey, you can't eat that. It's mine."

"Finders keepers," I said.

Kontos flipped the button on the remote and bed started to hum. Soon he was sitting up. "It's you isn't it?"

"Me what?" I hopped up on the end of the bed and sat cross legged. When he glared at me I shrugged. "It's not like you're using the whole length. I'm surprised they didn't put you in the children's ward."

"Don't change the subject. Finders Keepers, it's you, isn't it?"

"Maybe," I said, and unwrapped the second chocolate. "It's not exactly a secret."

"I knew it. That's why I got that weird email. *Panayia mou*, you're not going to tell anyone, are you?"

I thought about Kontos and his requests. Who could blame him for wanting to find love. Weren't we all looking for the same thing?

"No," I said after a moment. "I promise I won't tell anyone that Jimmy Kontos, porn star, wants to find a real live girlfriend so he can take long walks on the beach and drink pina coladas."

"You better not."

"Or what? You'll bite my ankles?" I looked over at his bedside table. A ball of green wool and two needles were perched on a stack of magazines. "Hey, what's with the knitting?

"I knit on the set. It keeps me relaxed while the fluffer does her job."

I was sorry I asked.

A sound at the door turned my head. Lydia was peering in.

"Allie, I thought I saw you walk by," she said. She was fresh-faced but looked like she'd been sort of a reverse Rip Van Winkle, awake for a hundred years.

"I didn't expect to see you up here." I glanced sideways at Kontos. He was practically drooling in his chocolate box. I rolled my eyes.

She leaned back in the doorway looked both ways before coming in.

"Have a seat," Kontos squeaked.

Lydia shook her head. "Can't stay. I'm here sitting with Eleni. I just wanted to thank you. Leo said that if it wasn't for you she'd probably be dead."

"How is she?"

"About the same."

That meant she still wasn't awake. Maybe she never would be.

"Have you been here all night?" I asked.

Lydia nodded.

"You want to go stretch your legs or go have a shower or something while I sit with her?"

"Thanks," she said almost shyly, something I hadn't seen in her before. "But I think I'll stay awhile. I don't think she has anyone else to care."

Right then and there I knew Lydia was a better person than me. Would I have forgiven someone who had rejected me, so readily? The answer was likely no.

All of a sudden an idea popped into my brain so hard that I very nearly slapped my forehead. How had I missed it?

I scribbled my cell phone number on a piece of paper and gave it to Lydia. "If you need me, call. I'd be happy to help you out."

"Thanks," she said, and pocketed the paper.

Kontos slapped me as soon as Lydia was gone. "Why didn't you get *her* number?"

"Why?"

"Because, she's hot, that's why."

I glared at him. "I'm not a lesbian."

"Not for you," he said. "For me."

I stood and stretched. The quiver had almost left my limbs. "You better talk to Leo," I told him. "He knows her better than I do."

"Yeah, okay," he said and picked up the phone.

Instead of flipping him off like I usually did, I waved. And he waved back. It was progress.

It was time to confront Olga's killer.

———

One lone player was left on the field.

With some trepidation, I peddled my bicycle to the front of one of the prettiest buildings on Merope. Within the walls of the massive stone house and its surrounding grounds, Merope's elderly residents checked in o Merope Springs when they needed extra care. Some came here by choice, and some came via an intervention by their families, but all needed that little bit of attention that just wasn't possible when you lived alone. It didn't look like a place where people came to eventually die.

People just like Kalliope Kefala.

"Kyria Eleni is in the hospital and requested that I come over and fetch her mother for an hour or so." I poised the pretty fountain pen over the visitors' book and prepared to write a phony name.

The receptionist consulted a list on her computer screen and looked at me with a bland expressionless face.

"That's not possible," she said, offering no further explanation.

"Because ..."

"She's not here."

This was like pulling teeth out of a crocodile. "Where is she?"

"She left for the hospital already. About ten minutes ago."

"You let a woman with dementia just leave on her own? What—did you give her the keys to your car, too?"

"No, she said, looking at me quizzically, "she has her own car. And she doesn't have dementia. Kyria Kefala is one of our healthiest residents."

CHAPTER TWENTY-SIX

Startled hospital staff gawked at me as I sprinted through the hallways. Nobody tried to stop me. Merope wasn't that kind of place. I bolted up the stairs two at a time, praying that I wouldn't trip. An old man wheeling an IV flipped me off as I skidded past him.

No time for payback.

Panting, I stumbled down the hallway. I passed Jimmy Kontas's room.

"Hey!" he called out, but I ignored him.

Eleni's room was at the end of the hall. The door was shut. I thrust the door open and entered.

Kalliope Kefala was already there, looking frail and lovely and clutching a pillow in on hand, her walking stick in the other. No sign of Lydia.

The box with the flashing lights continued to blip. Eleni was still alive. I relaxed a tiny bit.

"Where's Lydia?"

"The *putana*? I sent her home. I told her I wanted to look after my own daughter."

"Kyria Kefala, I don't think you want to do that."

She whirled around, still holding the flat hospital pillow. "This has nothing to do with you," she hissed.

"Actually, it kind of does." I took a deep breath, still trying to get air into my lungs after racing up three flights of stairs. "You killed my friend, so that makes it my business. And I can really hold a grudge, especially after you whacked me on the head--twice."

"I am not senile, girl. I only hit you once."

That was unexpected. "Where did you hit me then?"

Her expression was pure exasperation. "Where do you think I hit you?"

"Your daughter's house?"

"Yes, my daughter's house."

"With your walking stick?"

"A walking stick is a very useful thing to have."

That answered that question, although one whack remained unaccounted for, but I was starting to get an idea of who did it.

"She was going to tell you everything," Kyria Kalliope said.

"You mean that you killed Olga?"

"Olga bought this on herself. I told her--*begged her*--to keep that ... *girl* out of our lives. It was humiliating knowing my daughter had an illegitimate child out there. How would it look if everyone knew? Olga would not do it. She said the girl was old enough to make her own decisions, and if she wanted to contact Eleni, she could." Her laugh was the bright, clear tinkle of a perfectly sane person enjoying an amusing story at a tea party. "It was very easy. I just put my hands around Olga's throat and squeezed. And then she died. Knitting makes your fingers strong."

My heart fell and kept falling. Kyria Olga was killed over nothing, just one selfish, old woman's desire to save face.

"How did Eleni find out what you'd done."

Her laughter tinkled again. "Who do you think drove me there? We had been working in the garden when that nasty man called the house."

"Pavlos?"

Kyria Kalliope's nose wrinkled. "Such a crude man. Lucky thing I took the call. He wanted Eleni to own up to her sin. I had to do something, so I asked Eleni to take me to Olga's apartment to start setting things right. Of course my daughter got tired of waiting and came upstairs to get me, so she could not help but see what Olga had done to herself."

"What you did to her," I said.

"I told you: it was her fault. If she had told that girl to stay away from my family, Olga would be with us today. It is for the best. There will be no Olga Marouli to win the Winter Festival's knitting prize this year. That honor will go to me."

She sounded entirely too happy about the prospect.

A noise came from behind her. Eleni was stirring.

"Leave," the old lady hissed. "I have unfinished business with my daughter."

"Not a chance." I stepped toward her. "What about Pavlos? Why did you kill him?"

"I had to. He would not stop until everyone knew that he and Eleni had a child. I called him and asked him to meet me at the church. He was eager when I told him I had a proposition for him. Greedy, greedy man. I expect he thought I was going to pay him off. It was so easy to smack him on the head. No one will believe a delicate old lady was responsible."

Wow, a lot had happened after Shadow Guy helped me out. Kyria Kalliope had worked quickly while I was passed out around the corner.

My cellphone buzzed in my bag. My fingers inched toward it.

Kyria Kalliope nodded. "Go ahead an answer it. I have a thing to do."

Leo was on the other end. "The handwriting isn't a match to Eleni Kefala's."

"I know," I told him. "It's Maria Stamatou's. She's the one who hit me on the head at the old church."

"How--"

"Do you suppose we could do the conversation thing later? Right now you need to come to the hospital. I'm trying to fight a murderer here."

I ended the call and addressed the old lady with the death-pillow. "It's over, Kyria Kalliope. The police know and they're on their way over."

"How did you know it was me?"

"The dirt on Olga Marouli's face. After Eleni was attacked and eliminated I knew it had to be you. It wasn't just dirt, it was potting soil." At least I thought so.

"I knew I should have smacked you harder." She dropped the pillow and rushed at me, as fast as her artificial hips could carry her, swinging her walking stick in the air.

The door opened and Jimmy Kontos hobbled in. "Now you're picking on old ladies? What's next? Blind school children?"

Crash! The stick missed its target and smashed into the doorframe. She pulled back again and swung, this time smacking my bag. Virgin Mary, she sure was spry for an old duck.

"She's crazy!" Kontos yelled.

"No kidding. What are you doing in here?"

"I came looking for the blonde bowl of honey from earlier."

I dodged the third swing and crashed sideways into the IV stand. Eleni continued sleeping. Lucky cow.

I grabbed the pillow Kyria Kalliope had dropped and whacked her arm.

"That's for killing my friend." I hit her again. "And that's for hitting me with your old lady stick."

Her stick cracked across my knees. Tears stung my eyes. Walking sticks *hurt*.

Round and round the room we went, me leaping and darting to evade her stick. I could have used the pepper spray, but it would look bad if I sprayed an old lady, no matter that she was a homicidal kook.

Jimmy Kontos dropped down on the floor and rolled under the bed. "Ow! My stitches!"

"It's you own damn fault," I said, panting again. "Where's the nurse? Where's security?"

"This is a Greek hospital. Nobody cares unless you give them money to care."

Suddenly, there were noises in the hall outside. We both stopped to stare. Leo came sliding through door, Gus Pappas on his heels.

I flopped down in a chair, panting.

"You're under arrest for the murder of Pavlos Mavros and Olga Marouli," Leo said to the old woman.

She used her liver spotted hand as a fan. "Where am I? Who are you people?"

"*Skasmos,* Mama! Being a murderer is more humiliating than having a secret grandchild."

We all turned. Eleni Kefala was alive and awake.

————

Kyria Kalliope went willingly into police custody, but not without one final revelation. She had pancreatic cancer and would never see the inside of a courtroom, let alone a prison cell.

A hollow victory. Two people had died so an old lady could maintain her family's good name, and in the end it was pointless. The murders—and the murderer—made the cover of the country's newspapers. Everyone knew her motive was lame.

Eleni Kefala recovered quickly and was back home in her garden within days. Lydia respected her wishes and promised to stay away—for now.

Maria Stamatou admitted to running down Kyrios Moustakas, shooting Jimmy Kontos, and whacking me over the head at the church.

I was wrong; she looks fantastic in her prison jumpsuit.

The Maroulis clan went back to the mainland, but not without making sure they snubbed me completely when I said goodbye.

And Kyria Olga? She came to visit one last time. As soon as she appeared the look in her eyes told me this was goodbye.

Tears poured down my face as she thanked me.

"You have always been so good to me, and I will always love you like the nice child I never had. Now it is my turn to do something for you. Get out more, make some friends, and be happy."

"I'm a lone wolf, you know me." I brushed away the tears with the back of my hand.

"That is *skata*."

"I'll try," I blubbered.

"My girl." She hugged me tight with arms that felt solid and real.

"I have to go now, but I will always be with you. And for goodness sake, go and see Stavros. He needs to speak with you."

"I will."

Two days passed before I could muster up the wherewithal to leave the house. During that time my grief nearly crippled me. Lydia and Leo both came and went. Lydia, it turned out, was my new neighbor. Unbeknownst to me, Kyria Olga was the sole owner of the apartment building (and several others around the island) and divided her assets amongst her three grandchildren, leaving everything in trust for them until they reached a certain age. Her three children were bequeathed a small sum of money each, which they would forfeit if they contested the will.

Who knew?

Betty came with cupcakes. Lots of cupcakes. I ate them all. Toula brought brownies and frozen dinners. I ate those too. Jimmy Kontos sent over a selection of his movies. I shoved them in a box and hid them under the bed.

Eventually I showered, brushed my hair, and dressed in clean clothes. It was time to move on, and knowing that death wasn't the end made it a little easier. And so on that day I found myself at Stavros Psaris's house, doing what Kyria Olga had told me to do.

"I have been expecting you," he said when he opened the door. "I knew you'd come when you were ready."

"It's been rough," I told him honestly.

He nodded, his eyes telling me that he knew how I felt, and welcomed me into his home. Over coffee he revealed the other contents of Olga Marouli's will.

"The apartment you live in is yours. Olga had the paperwork drawn up and you own all four walls and everything inside."

I was too shocked to speak.

"She cared for you deeply." His eyes twinkled. "You were like one of her children, except that she actually enjoyed your company. That is not all."

"There's more?" I croaked.

"She left you her cat."

"Her cat?"

"A big marmalade cat. He died thirty-something years

ago, but apparently he has taken a liking to you. So she wants you to have him. I hear he does not eat too much these days."

My eyes widened in more shock. "How did you—"

Kyrios Stavros's laugh was warm. "You are not the only one who has a gift. I have visitors from time to time, including Olga."

I shook my head in disbelief. "All these years I thought I was alone."

"You are not alone."

I left in a daze, barely able to digest the information he'd given me. I owned my own place now, and I wasn't the only one the dead liked to chat to. The world felt a little less lonely.

The attitude of the Maroulis siblings was no surprise now, in light of the news I had just received. It was clear they hadn't responded warmly to the news that their mother was giving me my apartment, while they were given the slow, rotating inheritance-finger. They didn't leave empty-handed, but to them more was definitely, well, more.

———

Leo showed up that night with chocolate.

I took the box from his hands. "Are you trying to seduce me?"

"Yes." He followed me into the kitchen.

I leaned against the counter and studied him. "I thought I already told you it wasn't a good idea."

"I happen to think it's a great idea."

"Sex?"

"Sex ... and other things."

"How about dating?"

He moved closer. My pulse galloped. "Dating is good," he said.

"But not as good as sex?"

"I didn't say that." He slipped a hand behind my head and grabbed a handful of hair—not hard, but like he meant it—and tilted my head to one side. Then he leaned forward and nibbled gently.

A bonfire started in my pants.

"Can we do more of that if we date?" I asked, ready to pull off my clothes.

"We can do everything you want," he whispered against my neck and touched his tongue to the delicate skin.

I gulped. "Can we go on a date now?"

"Now?"

"Now."

He pulled away. "Go get ready. I'll be right here."

The future wasn't going to be perfect. Sooner or later I was going to have to tell Toula about me and Leo. I'd worry about that another time. Right now I had to get ready for a date.

ALSO BY ALEX A. KING